I0675348

THE WRATHFUL CUP OF SCORN

A Carcassonne Medieval Mystery

E. A. RIVIÈRE

Copyright © 2021 by E. A. Rivière

All rights reserved. No part of this publication may be reproduced, distributed or transmitted in any form or by any means, including photocopying, recording, or other electronic or mechanical methods, without the prior written permission of the author, except in the case of brief quotations embodied in critical reviews and certain other noncommercial uses permitted by copyright law.

This is a work of fiction. Names, characters, places, and incidents are a product of the author's imagination. Locales and public names are sometimes used for atmospheric purposes. Any resemblance to actual people, living or dead, or to businesses, companies, events, institutions, or locales is completely coincidental.

Cover Illustration © 100 Covers

Book Layout: David Pasquantonio

The Wrathful Cup of Scorn/E. A. Rivière—1st ed.

ISBN 978-1-7372892-4-1

For

Ullie
light of my life

and

Moog
wise counselor

Carcassonne (now southern France), the year 1200

CHAPTER I.

Bertwoin Teisseire and his youngest sister, Maud, were resting in the shade under an elm tree when the pig-killer came swaggering out of the forest. They both rose to face Perter Sabatier, and Maud took half a step backwards to stand behind her big brother.

Bertwoin wasn't sure he would win a fight with the surly butcher, who was shorter but had a muscled body matted with dark hair, though he could probably hold him off long enough for Maud to run home and fetch help. But he would have to stay alert. The pig-man took pleasure in smacking people's heads and in slitting the tough throats of trusting pigs.

Why had he come to their farm? Bertwoin then noticed that Perter carried a hand sickle and relaxed. The butcher's mother-in-law, Éléonore, had borrowed it from them. She must have asked him to return it.

"I brought back your tool," Perter said, his tone implying they were rude to want it back. "We had to sharpen it."

"About time," Bertwoin said. "Pa was thinking of asking you to pay rent on it."

Perter grunted and said, "Don't sass your elders." He surveyed their farm with a shrewd and knowing eye.

The sky was the color of bronze, and the wheat fields rippled like linen sheets ruffled by the wind. Bertwoin stood up straighter. Much of the work done within sight was his doing. His father had held onto and expanded their farm with his fists and his cunning, but Bertwoin had dug out the stumps, plowed these fields, and primed the black soil for growth. Like their steadfast mules, Left and Right, years of his sweat had watered the thirsty ground.

Perter turned his attention to ten-year-old Maud, half-hidden behind her brother, and his smile became smug and loathsome. "I've got a rabbit that needs carried up to the chateau keep."

"There's nobody here right now who can run your errands for you," Bertwoin said.

"Not very neighborly of you. There might be a bit of pork in it for you."

"Maud still has to clabber the milk, and I need to go cut reeds in the marshland. But I'll tell Pa of your offer when he comes back. Maybe he'll send someone over to carry the rabbit for you."

"If it's not done right now, then my offer's taken back. Lazing about under an elm tree gets nothing done."

Bertwoin grinned. "If our resting a moment bothers you, you can tell Pa about it."

Perter looked ready to butcher Bertwoin with the sickle he held. "You're a sassy pup, ain't you? Think you're better than the rest of us because your pa's an ex-crusader and the alchemist used you to help solve a murder. You'd best make sure no one runs over your tail with their wheel." He tossed the sickle at Bertwoin's feet and stomped away like a peeved child.

When he picked up the tool, Bertwoin saw a threadlike

crack in its oak handle. His father would hold Perter accountable for the damage, even though Éléonore had borrowed the sickle.

"I don't like him," Maud said.

"That makes you part of a large crowd. He gets along better with pigs than people."

"He slapped me once."

"What? When?"

"Not long after Papa made him apologize for clubbing Wilfraed."

"Why'd he smack you?"

"He didn't like an answer I gave him. Said I was being uppity like everyone else in my family."

Bertwoin watched the sturdy pig-tender march out of sight in the woods and rubbed the knuckles of his right fist. "You never said anything about it."

"He told me never to tell anyone."

Bertwoin sucked in his bottom lip. "Maybe we should let it stay that way. It'll be our secret. If you tell Pa, he might break Perter's arm. And if the pig-killer can't work, then those who depend on him don't eat. Éléonore and her family nearly starved when he ran off to the mountains to avoid Pa."

Bertwoin scratched his chin and stared at the trees where Perter had disappeared. Of course, the pig-killer had to be punished, but not by their father. Bertwoin wasn't certain he would win a face-to-face fight against the sturdy butcher, so he would do it on the sly.

BERTWOIN FIDGETED AS HE SAT WAITING IN AMBUSH BEHIND prickly gorses, their yellow flowers luminous under the brash moonlight. The air was damp and smelled of the Aude River with minnows flicking in the reeds and fish sliding up under them to feed. He kept watch over a deserted road laid down by Roman slaves only eighty years after legionaries had crucified Jesus for unholy reasons in the Holy Land.

The master alchemist had told Bertwoin that those who now rode or walked this road should thank a swaggering Roman consul for ordering it built. The consul had been notorious for parading about the generous green countryside on the gray back of a ponderous war elephant…and now over a thousand years later, folks remembered the legendary beast, not its pompous rider. They even remembered its name: Domitius.

The elephant's ghost was still sometimes seen lumbering eastward on the road, doomed to roam riderless in the eerie cleft between the past and present. Bertwoin longed to see the pale brute, but he also feared to meet it.

He scratched itches and sat on his calves—an uncomfortable position—so he wouldn't fall asleep. Luckily, he could hear a minstrel play tunes on a tin pipe at Tisbe's rude tavern, the music frolicking across the gaunt fields. Torches guttered and their flames wavered in the tavern yard, drawing revelers like night insects to their light. The grunting pig-killer roistered among them, not knowing that a headache awaited him.

Bertwoin decided he would never become a bandit. Cleaning latrines was less boring than waiting in ambush at night. And where was Perter? Had he taken a different road home?

His father should have given the pig-tender a beating instead of accepting his public apology at the Sunday market. Then maybe the butcher wouldn't have felt smug enough afterwards to smack Maud. You couldn't be merciful with his kind.

Perter had come two months before with the *bayle* to arrest Bertwoin after Emeline's mutilated corpse was discovered floating face-down in the sinewy Aude River. During the arrest, Perter, whose temperament was ever peevish, had cudgeled Bertwoin's brother, Wilfraed, for no fit reason. Wilfraed had suffered eye-watering headaches until the pain divinely disappeared after he attended Sunday mass.

When Bertwoin's father, Clanoud, had vowed to wrench the pig-butcher's elbow out of joint in revenge, Perter fled south to lofty mountain crags and thin-air summer pastures.

He eventually hiked back down to their blustering marketplace where he had begged forgiveness for his sin, an act that soothed his father's bristly pride. He also had agreed to butcher their winter meat for them.

But shaming the pig-bleeder in public, which glorified the father's power more than it atoned for the blow given Wilfraed, didn't satisfy Bertwoin. He had vowed then to repay Perter's cruelty in kind, a blow for a blow. And he was one to keep his promises, even if they were only private ones made to himself.

Besides, Bertwoin didn't doubt that the smug pig-butcher had puffed out his hairy chest and bragged at Tisbe's tavern about the skull-bashing he had given one of Clanoud's sons. Other louts might come to believe they too could knock Wilfraed about and just apologize for it later.

But where was the oaf ? Since Perter had smacked Wilfraed's skull with a wooden spoke, Bertwoin had secretly borrowed a broken spoke from a wheelwright's workplace. The sacred law of "eye for eye, tooth for tooth" demanded exact revenge.

Bertwoin hoped the pig-killer came staggering home alone. He would have prayed to the Virgin Mary for this boon if his intention had been less of a sin. He knew he should turn the other cheek, as the Blessed Savior demanded; but Montredon, his practical village, was given more to Old Testament justice than to the catechism of love. They respected not the taking of a blow so much as the giving of it.

Besides, did not even the pious Pope keep an army that was more inclined to stab and bash his enemies than to bestow holy forgiveness on them?

Poplars near Bertwoin rustled as if they shared his restless impatience. A sweet sycamore, fragrant as a noblewoman, perfumed the breeze. He pulled the neck of his woolen tunic tighter. Above him, the moon resembled an onion cut in half, and he kept his eyes averted because some said the hungry moon could leech away a man's sanity.

Bertwoin heard the murmur of a voice not twenty paces away and raised into a squat, ready to spring out from behind the thorny gorse bushes. He hoped to see Perter staggering home half-drunk on brown ale, mumbling and singing to himself.

Instead, two barefoot men wearing black robes with leather thongs for belts ghosted past him. Their furtive manner made the backs of Bertwoin's upper arms crimp with gooseflesh. He made the sign of the holy cross as they glided along in determined silence, their uncanny dignity making the tavern shouts and hoots booming across the night seem rude. Though they swept past like spirits, he knew they were Good Folk weavers, probably on their way to preach their creed somewhere or minister to someone who lay dying.

Bertwoin again sat on his aching calves and shins, took a bit of hard goat cheese from his pouch, and savored its gamy flavor. He expected to hear the pig-killer come grunting along the rumpled road even if he wasn't muttering or singing.

When would the lout come? The half-moon was already straight overhead.

A woman's whine startled him. He rose into a squat with the broken spoke in hand. If it was Perter, he wasn't alone; he had his young wife, Alesta, with him. Bertwoin tied a woolen cloth over his nose and mouth so she couldn't hide his face.

Two shadows emerged from the darkness and became

distinct bodies walking in the moonlight. The gruff pig-butcher stomped down the middle of the road between the ruts, dragging Alesta along by a thin arm. She took jerky steps to stay upright while pulling against his bruising grip.

"Shut up, you spoiled brat," Perter snarled.

At Tisbe's tavern, a woman sang a throaty love lament in tune with a minstrel's piping. She wasn't singing about Alesta's marriage. There was lament there, but not love. Bertwoin figured living with Perter was purgatory on the good days, hell on the others.

"Not this road. Not at night," Alesta whined. "Let's go the other way. The elephant might stomp on me."

"You'll do what I tell you to do, or you'll regret the day your *maman* whelped you. Force me to drag you all the way home, little bitch, and I'll whip you 'til blood runs down your runty legs."

Perter and Alesta reached the gorse bushes. Bertwoin hesitated. Should he wait for another night when the pig-killer stumbled home alone? He had no intention of confronting the bully and fighting him with fists or knives. The contrary ass-crack had struck Wilfraed without warning, and the sacred law of the Old Testament called for exact revenge. Besides, if Perter didn't see him, he couldn't accuse him of assault. And Alesta might not recognize him with a cloth over his nose.

"If the elephant stomps on me," she whimpered, "I'll be squashed like a wine grape. We shouldn't be out here after dark. Nobody else is."

The pig-killer smacked her cheek, grabbed her hair, and jerked her head backward, snarling down into her face. "The Devil himself won't bother you while I'm with you. Do what I say, or I'll come down hard on you." He slapped her pouty face again. "I'm not going to argue words no more. Now get along."

"You can beat me here and now," she growled, her manner changed, "but you'll regret it someday."

Perter hesitated and muttered, "Don't threaten me, ass meat." He slapped her face a third time but with less force.

The pig-killer glanced behind him at the tavern where the woman still crooned of her hero's love. Bertwoin watched Alesta. She cringed in front of her brutish husband, sobbing, probably with the taste of sweet blood in her mouth.

Bertwoin thought of his little sister with her twiggy arms and legs. Had she also tasted blood? The whoreson pig-killer was meaner than Satan's cat. He deserved his punishment now.

Bertwoin slipped out of his hiding place silent as a fox and tiptoed toward the angry pig-sticker. Alesta saw him creeping up behind her husband. Her eyes widened, shining in the moonlight like two weak fireflies.

Seeing her sudden fear, Perter started to turn. Bertwoin whacked him across the temple with the spoke, its sound that of a wet cloth slapping the side of a wooden bucket. Perter fell loose-limbed and slack-jawed to his knees.

For a sickening moment, Bertwoin thought he might have broken the pig-killer's skull bone, but Perter moaned and hunched over on his knees with his head cradled in his arms. His straw hat had fallen off, and one could see a dark stain of blood spread on the white coif over his hair.

Alesta pulled her knife and glared at him with righteous hatred, her teeth bared like a wolf protecting her cub. She stood beside her moaning husband to prevent a second blow. At least, she hadn't screamed and raised the rabble at the tavern. Bertwoin silently thanked her for that.

He slapped the broken spoke in his free hand and explained, "He hits people just out of meanness."

"Out of meanness? That's not why he did it, furrow-hopper. Ask your father why my husband smacked your brother. Ask your heartless father why he's no better than the *visconte's* seneschal."

Bertwoin flinched. She recognized him. Now the *bayle* would come after him. But there was little he could do about that now.

"My father?" What offense had his irascible father committed against Perter? How was he the same as Sir Jean-Luc, the young *visconte's* powerful seneschal?

"Well, it's done now," he said.

"Is it, Ox?" she said, using his nickname. "Is it not my husband's turn now to take revenge against you?" She pointed at his belly with her knifepoint. "He gave one blow and received two in return."

"I only hit him once."

She sniffed, her expression ridiculing his stupidity. "The first blow was your righteous father shaming him in public. The second was your cowardly blow from behind."

"He also hit my sister." Bertwoin chopped the air with one hand. "This was men's business, and it's now done."

One side of her lips curled upward. "So the men are finished? Then it's women's business now. Let's see if your mother can protect her ox."

Was she going to report him to the *bayle*, the formidable lawman who worked for Sir Jean-Luc? Or did she mean Perter would revenge this blow? He turned and strode away.

There was little use now in dodging into the forest to avoid meeting anyone who might see him carrying the broken wheel spoke. He didn't have to risk the imps and demons that hunted the night woods. Instead, he began to trek cross-country over the harvested fields toward Montredon.

When the *bayle* had come three months before to arrest him for Emeline's murder, Bertwoin had fled into the woods, hidden there, then gone to the master alchemist for help.

This time he wouldn't hide. He would accept his punishment, a whipping or public shaming.

Had he been stupid to be so impatient? Why had he not waited to strike Perter until he was alone? Now the pig-sticker would come for him with the might and the right of the law behind him. Well, there was no changing that now.

How had Alesta recognized him? Of course, she had noticed his plowman's shoulder. His left one was twisted a bit higher than the right one and this marked him as a furrow-cutter, as she had called it.

At least this night, the pig-sticker would take home a headache in return for the one he had bestowed upon Wilfraed and also to revenge his slapping Maud. There was satisfaction in that, or there should have been.

He didn't feel content. Was Alesta right? Had Perter already been punished enough, and if so, why had he taken it as *his* duty to also punish the butcher? Ah well, the pig-killer was a brute and deserved the blow, but Alesta and her mother, Éléonore, didn't deserve the trouble he had just laid on them. After all, he had just wounded their breadwinner.

Bertwoin shrugged. Done was done. Tomorrow at sunrise, he needed to slip into the wheelwright's outdoor shed and return the broken spoke.

He wouldn't argue against Alesta when she accused him. He would instead announce why he had assaulted the pig-sticker and accept the official punishment laid on him. After-ward, his father would punish him for not accepting his deci-sion that Perter's public apology excused the blow he had given Wilfraed. At least, everyone would now know that attacking anyone in his family meant receiving punishment in return.

CHAPTER II

Three days later, Perter stepped back from the gaping carcass of a bristly boar he was butchering in the château's forecourt and grunted. Good, only a few people carrying produce and poultry and grain nodded to him, wanting him to notice them. Word had already gone around the hearth fires that an angel had blessed him.

He rinsed sticky gore off his hands in a bucket of water, washed his long knife clean, slipped it into his leather belt, and laid his blood-slicked, leather apron aside on a stool.

Putting on a bored expression, Perter ambled into the late autumn glare bouncing off an East Gate tower and stopped to survey the large courtyard with its row of elms in the middle aflutter with starlings. People only gave him a curious glance before attending to their own business.

He strayed to the keep, forming the south side of the forecourt, and sauntered along its rough-hewn wall to the kitchen's arched doorway tucked away in the far corner like a mouse hole. Standing off to one side, he peeked into Chef Arundel Vidal's domain. Two sweating bellows boys pumped fires red hot for two grill cooks who fried meat in the soot-blackened pits, an old woman filleted a salmon fit for a duke, a younger woman sitting on a stool tore feathers from a limp-necked duck, two strong spit boys turned large cuts of pork, and other kitchen workers bustled about active as bees.

The usually vigilant Arundel worked at a scarred table in the kitchen's middle, blind to everything around him as he sprinkled grated nutmeg onto a thick green sauce. He stirred his precious sauce with a spoon, a wooden one because the touch of metal might taint its taste, or so he said. The chef's dish of creamed sorrel sauce poured over pork sausage was famous as far away as Aragon and always brought him compliments. Once, rumor had it, this sauce had even brought him an offer to cook for a duke. Too bad the puffed-up soup-maker hadn't taken the offer.

Perter had heard that today three nobles from Catalonia were visiting. *Visconte* Raimon-Rogièr and his seneschal, Sir Jean-Luc, hoped a delicious meal would sink their visitors into contentment and make trade negotiations flow easy as a river.

Perter smiled at the clang and clatter echoing off the narrow kitchen's walls. Arundel supervised his kitchen each day as if he were managing a small military campaign. He had skill, no one could gainsay that, but his manner was as arrogant as a strutting rooster. He acted as if a night angel had singled *him* out. Well, maybe his reputation was about to go sour.

Perter sniffed at the delicious fog of braised meat, cloves, and cinnamon that scented the kitchen, though its odor seemed faint to him. The pig's blood splattered on his beard and mustache clotted his sense of smell.

Everything was as it should be. As he had hoped, everyone was busy. Still, passing through the kitchen to trespass into the larder was too risky. He had no more right to visit the closet than a fox does to sneak into a pigeon loft. So he cruised back down the rough wall of weathered stones to the keep's main door and dodged inside it.

Perter drifted through the dark warmth of the cavernous, high-ceilinged room with its stone staircase and large stone fireplace and crossed behind a woman in a grass-green tunic who was down on her knees, scrubbing the flagstone floor. He glanced back from a small doorway ablaze with sunlight before going out. She hadn't bothered to notice him.

Perter grunted. Why did those who work always find themselves on their knees for the nobility and the Church? He stepped out into the *Cour du Midi*, the narrow courtyard where those in the château feasted when the weather allowed dining outside.

Rows of trestle tables stood silent and ready with red-and-white cloths draped over them, the colors celebrating the Trencavel coat of arms. Benches lined the tables. Goblets, trenchers of old bread, and forks stood ready for the feasters.

As expected, the courtyard was quiet and empty. No one loitered among the tables, no one who might shoo him away, or try to since he wasn't one to obey a servant, especially now after he had been touched by an angel. Had the angel bestowed the gift of luck on him? Surely some benefit must come from a heavenly visit. So far all he had gotten was a thumping headache.

A gust scurried across the tabletops, ruffling the hanging sides of the linen cloths. Perter coughed, the chesty sound hollow as if it rose out of a deep barrel.

Arundel's kitchen had a door leading into a small larder with an opposite door leading onto the bright *Cour du Midi*. Perter peeked through this open door and saw no one in the closet, so he ducked inside. The larder door leading into the kitchen was open, but everybody was too busy to notice him, so he swung it shut and dropped its crossbar in place. Now no one could surprise him.

Some of the shelves inside the larder were already laden with food and drink for those fortunate enough to dine today with young *Visconte* Raimon-Rogièr and *Viscontesse* Agnes. A shelf stacked with clay pitchers and bowls for wine and ale also had a single pewter tankard on it. Its base displaying the stamped image he sought: a pagan beast with the crouching body of a lion and the predatory head and wings of an eagle. This tankard belonged to Sir Jean-Luc's son, Master Servay, who insisted on drinking a syrupy apple cider brought especially for him from the abbey in Saint-Papoul. The cider had already been brought from the cellar and poured out so as not to interfere with the last-minute duties of serving the feast.

Perter grunted. So the brat thought himself too good to drink what was set out on the tables in common bowls. Well, he had made it easy, hadn't he? Let Sir Jean-Luc pace the château's corridors with worry while his son lay abed afire with a fever that lasted for days. Let him feel the vengeance of "eye for eye, tooth for tooth."

Again Perter felt the need to cough. He suppressed it so no suspicious sound came from the larder, though no one working in the noisy kitchen would probably hear it. Still, better wise caution than being caught.

Perter pulled a clay vial from a hidden pocket sewn into his tunic, unstoppered it, and poured the dark berry juice it contained into the sweet cider. Let Master Servay have his fill and retch like a poisoned rat. He'd remember this meal for the rest of his days.

Before sneaking back to the open *Cour du Midi*, Perter found another goblet on another shelf stamped with the same pagan beast, only larger. Raising his tunic bottom, he fouled the goblet's top rim by rubbing it around in his pungent crotch. It belonged to Sir Jean-Luc. Unlike the monster that signified the seneschal's family, the base of the *visconte's* goblet was marked with the noble image of a lion, a beast one could honor because it didn't defy nature.

Perter unbarred the larder door leading to the kitchen, then hurried back down the empty *Cour du Midi* to the keep's entrance room. The woman scrubbing the floor again ignored him. This, of course, pleased him.

He moseyed back to the boar's carcass hung on the butchering rack set up in the château's forecourt. There he cut and wrestled the right shoulder off of the pig, meat worthy of being served at the high table because it came from the animal's right side.

Perter toted the fresh meat to the kitchen and stopped just inside the doorway a moment to gloat. Soon the day would fall face down for the arrogant chef who thought himself pure gold compared to peasants. Let strutting Arundel explain to Sir Jean-Luc and the young *visconte* how Master Servay came to be sick after drinking and eating what the chef had served him.

As he carried the shoulder meat to a stone shelf near one of the three open hearths built into a wall, a few workers glanced up from their clay dishes or bubbling pots or iron spits. The hag renowned for her skill in baking trout smiled at the hemp-cloth bandage under his straw hat and widened her eyes in mock amazement. Arundel laughed and put his hands up as if praying to Perter for a boon. His sorrel sauce finished and probably tasting delicious, the wiry chef now seemed in a playful mood.

Perter snarled at the haughty bastard who padded about with the confidence of a nobleman's favorite greyhound. His anger caused the ass-crack to laugh even more.

Then the lordly chef saw a bellows boy snatch a few almonds off an oak table in the center of the hot kitchen as he walked past it. Arundel grabbed a long spoon, charged after the boy, and smacked the side of his head. Didier yelped and clutched his ear. He flinched away, putting his back toward the chef to protect his head from a second blow.

"You don't pinch-poach in here," Arundel bellowed, snapping the spoon against the palm of his empty hand to emphasize each word. He glared around the room like an outraged gander to make certain everyone understood his clay-tablet kitchen law.

For a held breath, his workers stood frozen, then the old fish cook started dicing an onion again, her knife snicking on a wooden board. The others relaxed and returned to what they were doing before their chef's imperious outburst.

Arundel turned back to Perter and eyed the hemp-cloth bandage under his brimmed hat. "Perter the Touched," he mocked. "Maybe if you lay a hand on our heads, we too will partake of the angel's blessing."

Perter deliberately pinched a sliver of raw meat off of the shoulder he had brought inside and chewed it in front of the chef, daring him to try and slap his ear.

"Why do you need my help, master chef ? Are you not one who also bestows blessings?" Perter patted the shoulder meat. "Is it not a rare honor for this boar to have its flesh boiled and roasted by the famous Arundel? Oh Lord, yes, you bring these animals lasting glory. They are *honored* to sacrifice their bodies for your meals. You make them delicious. You make them fit to pass through noble stomachs on their way to their final resting places in château privies. The saints we celebrate would think themselves blessed if fed by you."

Arundel picked up a butcher's knife as long as his forearm and made a point of waiting for the pig-man to leave his kitchen. Perter shrugged and strutted out into the bright courtyard, chuckling at Arundel's anger. Soon the famous chef would have a bigger problem than Didier palming a few almonds. He would have to explain why he had sickened Master Servay.

CHAPTER III

Didier carried a pot of succulent rabbit stew to the serving closet. His ear, as well as his pride, still ached.

As he set the stew on a shelf in the larder, his eye fell on the tankard full of cider set aside especially for Master Servay, the seneschal's haughty son.

More spiced cider was due from the Saint-Papoul Abbey tomorrow. If this juice went missing, there would be no time to fetch more ere the meal began. Master Servay would then have to make do and drink common ale or young wine. Master Servay was sure to throw a tantrum like a spoiled three-year-old. Arundel would have to answer for not having the cider ready at hand.

Didier smiled. His prank would stoke Arundel like a hearth fire. And the chef would rage even more when he found that like the cider, his bellows boy with a sore ear was also missing. Didier had little liking for the cramped, hot work of puffing up fires all day. He preferred the more solitary labor of watching sheep graze in open-air pastures, migrating first to the mountains, then to the lowlands.

Besides, this was his best chance to embarrass the bully chef. Other kitchen workers, one or two anyway, would laugh all winter at his revenge.

Didier stepped into a shadowy corner of the larder and gulped down the sweet cider. He burped, set the tankard back with its lid down so its emptiness might not be discovered until the last moment, then slipped out of the larder. As soon as someone discovered that the tankard was empty, he would disappear.

Not long afterward while Didier pumped air into a fire under a beet soup bubbling in the middle hearth, a sudden shaft of light pierced his eyes like a sword thrust into his brain. The front of his skull felt heavy; and without warning, his face felt feverish, hot. His vision blurred. He staggered toward a stone shelf recessed in the wall, desperate to reach the water jug on it and wet his parched throat.

Everyone stared at him, their faces blurry. Arundel yelled for him to get out, which would have made him laugh if he wasn't hurting. Water! He needed water. A fire blazed in his throat.

He fell to his knees three steps before reaching the shelf. The light coming in from the courtyard doorway stabbed into his skull. His muscles twitched, and his crotch turned warm and wet.

Someone yelled, the sound echoing in his head. A boogeyman, Arundel, bent over him, his face goatish, his features grotesquely distorted. It didn't surprise him. He had always thought the chef might be a devil disguised as a person.

FEAR ICED THROUGH ARUNDEL. HE KNEW THE DEADLY signs of poison when he saw them. Had Didier pinched-poached more food while no one was looking? What now? He must dodge all guilt. He needed to save his kitchen and keep his reputation blameless.

He would claim that unknown to him Didier had been sick. No one outside of his kitchen must know about the boy's thieving. No one must think the poison came from his food.

But was there even now tainted sauce or corrupt meat among the dishes ready to be served? He had no time to prepare all the food and drink again, yet he had no idea what Didier had eaten or drunk. Why did this have to happen now when they had important guests?

He must find the poison. For that, he needed the château steward to assign him tasters.

Arundel sent a scullion running to the steward, though he expected the strutting prig to be testy about coming. He would probably ignore his request. But the arrogant bastard would dance as he was told to do and learn who had real power in a situation like this.

While he waited, Arundel had Didier's body laid along the back wall and covered with a canvas tarp.

The steward sent Arundel's scullion back, as expected, with the peevish message that he was far too busy serving the needs of the *visconte's* eminent guests to come running to the kitchen. The chef was to solve his own problems.

Arundel told the boy, "Go back and tell the steward that if he doesn't get his ass down here immediately, there will be no feast today. And tell him that all the blame will fall on his witless head."

As expected, the scowling steward soon rushed into the kitchen, his expression already dismissive. "Don't ever give me orders again, cook. I'm not a dog to be brought to heel."

Arundel pointed a commanding finger at the covered corpse lying on the floor at the back of the room.

The steward scowled at the bundle, no doubt guessing from its shape that a body lay there. "What the…?"

Arundel raised a dictatorial hand to silence the steward, then motioned for a spit boy to pull back the canvas tarp over the body. When Didier's lax body was exposed, the chef said, "You will immediately have this body removed so the guests don't know he died here. Then I want four of your lesser servants sent here to act as tasters. Do it now if you want your feast when *Visconte* Raimon-Rogièr orders it served."

Arundel turned away, strode to the nearest hearth, and lifted the lid on a pot to check its contents. The steward was dismissed. It was now his problem to solve.

To salvage some of his self-esteem, the steward said to Arundel's back. "We'll talk more on this later." He then rushed out into the forecourt.

PERTER HAD JUST GUTTED A SUCKLING PIG AND SET ASIDE its heart, liver, lungs, and kidneys when three men hauled a canvas tarp out of the kitchen. The shape of the burden inside it suggested a corpse. His stomach went weightless as if he were falling out of a tree. Had Master Servay drunk some of the cider? Had Éléonore's poison gone wrong, or had she really meant to kill the seneschal's son?

He had assumed she merely wanted to sicken Master Servay and put the fear of retribution into the seneschal. But Éléonore had never said she wouldn't kill the brat. And she *was* almost insane with grief. Her boy had died, and she believed Sir Jean-Luc could have saved him. So why shouldn't his son not also die?

Perter grunted. If found guilty of this crime, he would be tortured, then hung. His precious neck would feel the choking clamp of a rope while his feet scrabbled in the air for something solid to stand on.

Had Arundel or a kitchen worker sampled the cider to make certain it hadn't soured? No, surely the poison wasn't strong enough for a simple sip to kill a grown man or woman. Master Servay must have slipped in early to slake his thirst.

When the steward led a cluster of servants into the kitchen, Perter carried the suckling pig to the kitchen door. All the workers were overly intent on what they were doing; they looked like scolded dogs. He lugged the suckling inside and dropped it on a table.

"Who'd they carry out?" he asked a spit boy working the nearest hearth.

The boy glanced at Arundel, saw he was busy, and whispered, "Didier."

So it was the bellows boy Arundel had smacked on the ear. Had the cook hit him too hard? Or had Didier decided to repay the chef for the blow he had received?

"How'd he die?"

"Poison."

So Didier had drunk part or all of Master Servay's cider to embarrass the chef. The boy had no more brains than a gnat. Arundel would have punished him until he whimpered for mercy.

Well, at least now he knew Éléonore's revenge, though spoiled this time, would go far beyond just sickening the seneschal's brat.

He stretched his back and grunted. Half amused, he watched Arundel take four servants, two men and two women, around the tables laden with food and have them take turns tasting different dishes. The chef asked what they thought as if he wanted their opinions on the food's flavors instead of waiting to see if one of them fell dead at his feet.

The kitchen workers, still looking guilty as dogs, watched the servants without appearing to do so.

Had Didier drunk all of the deadly cider? If not, then one of the tasters was about to follow Didier to Hell. He didn't want to be in the kitchen when that happened.

Still, he might drop the chef into a puddle of piss before he left or even stop the tasting. "Arundel," he called out, "whose body was that they just carried out? Who did your kitchen poison?"

The chef rushed at him, pausing only to pick up a long knife. "Out, ass-crack. Out!"

Perter also grabbed a knife off a table and stood his ground. "Are those the food testers?" he asked and pointed his chin at the two men and two women.

The four duped servants looked stricken.

Little Arundel glanced back at his tasters to determine the damage done. Perter retreated, tossing the kitchen knife on a small table beside the door.

If there was some Saint-Papoul cider left in the pagan-marked tankard, Master Servay might yet catch his death. If not, Éléonore would want to try again. Her grief made her as wrathful as a spurned witch.

In the meantime, he would go about his business and tell everyone he met that the château's kitchen was poisoning people. That would tie a knot in haughty Arundel's rat tail.

CHAPTER IV.

For five days, Bertwoin roamed the sheltering forest, carrying a long beechwood stick. The grapes were harvested, wine-making was in progress, and the autumn plowing done; it was time for him to fatten the lean, long-legged pigs for winter meat. As he knocked acorns and beech mast from overhead limbs, he kept watch for the relentless *bayle*.

When the lawman didn't come to arrest him, Bertwoin decided to stop hiding in the woods. So on the sixth morning, he again marched into the forest after breakfast with a grunting entourage of eager swine; but once he was out of his stern father's sight, he leaned his stick against an oak tree and sneaked away to visit Flowia, the alchemist's assistant known as the "virgin" for some unknown reason.

The piggy faces around him full of hope made Bertwoin feel guilty, but not guilty enough to forgo visiting Flowia. He smiled at the thought of her seeing him arrive with an entourage of grunting swine.

Flowia might know why the *bayle* hadn't come for him. The alchemist encouraged her to listen to local gossip so he knew what folks believed and how they felt. She might know why Perter hadn't grabbed this easy chance for revenge against Bertwoin and his family. After all, it cost him nothing but a trip to the *bayle*. It was then the lawman's duty to confront him and his unpredictable father.

Then again, maybe Perter *had* complained to the *bayle* after Alesta told her husband who had clubbed him. Then why had the lawman decided to ignore the charge? Did he think this petty dispute not worth his time, especially since the loutish butcher had brought this trouble down upon his own shoulders by striking Wilfraed?

Or did the *bayle* hesitate because of the unspoken bond between him and his father? They had faced and fought the deadly Moors together at Acre and Jaffa during the last crusade. They had marched together as comrades far from home. Bertwoin smirked. To remind everyone of his warrior days, the *bayle* wore a bold scarlet rood stitched across the chest of his horse-leather tunic.

The *bayle* also knew that even with the *visconte* and seneschal's authority behind him, gruff Clanoud might go berserk during an arrest. His father was quick to use his fists. The war still afflicted him, body and mind, and the wounds and scars that wormed his wiry body disgruntled his temper. Sometimes his wounds just ached, other times they pricked him like falling into a thorn bush. Nightmares haunted his sleep. He had returned from the Holy Land more demon-possessed than God-inspired.

Bertwoin's *maman* said it was a miracle his father wasn't an outlaw tending sheep in some far-off mountain pasture. He had killed two men since returning from the Holy Land and maimed one disrespectful cobbler, all done, of course, in the name of self-defense. The shoe-mender only remained alive because three strong men and his courageous wife—swinging a wooden mallet—had intervened in the brawl.

Would his father find out that he had slipped away to see Flowia? His father hadn't out-and-out forbidden him to visit her, which was surprising because his father's snarling disgust for her was as clear as water. He believed his son was betraying him. His son was smitten with a young woman whose veins flowed with the poisoned blood of the Moors. Everyone in his household—his Uncle Laurence especially—hated her. How could he convince them that loving her was not treason against the family? And on the other side, how could he ever coax stubborn Flowia into accepting his domineering father?

But today he need not worry about that. As he hiked through the woods, he plucked a few leaves of mint and chewed them to sweeten his breath. Already half of the disappointed pigs had wandered away to forage for themselves. Those still with him seemed confused, their expressions worried. Nuts weren't pattering down from the trees.

A breeze sizzled through the foliage, and a few clouds white as goose down feathered the yellow October sky. Bertwoin's blood quickened and surged through him like spring sap. He was going to see Flowia, who was wise in the ways of plants and love.

He ducked under a tree limb speckled with sunlight and smiled at the memory of the *bayle* coming to arrest him two months earlier for Emeline's foul murder. The lawman's coming had brought him a blessing as well as trouble. When he had fled to the master alchemist for help, he had met and later formed a bond with Flowia.

Nearing the alchemist's cottage, Bertwoin skipped a few steps and raised his arms in exuberant joy. The two stubborn pigs still following him glanced skyward as if Saint Bertwoin might rain sweet acorns down from the sun-radiant heavens.

Magpies glided and sported on the wind, reflecting his feelings. He laughed as he watched them dance in the air.

Flowia stood inside the mulberry hedge surrounding the poultry yard with a dead goose laid out on a portable table in front of her. His stomach gurgled. It was a "green goose," not having the heft and fatness of one kept alive until the Christmas feast, but its meat would be tender.

Normally a few geese patrolled the poultry yard. The first to see him would honk to warn the others of his presence… but not today. The yard was empty of live geese. Maybe it was too painful to watch Flowia rip feathers off a limp brother or sister.

She wore a brown woolen apron over a long, blue dress and had tied a square of white lace over her black hair, which hung down to her waist in a single, thick braid. A growl of lust tingled through his groin.

But blast his luck, Flowia was not alone. The wise woman called Ugly Thea stood beside the table. He had to choose his words with care. Some said she could hear people's thoughts. She wasn't called ugly because of her physical appearance but because her temper turned ugly when someone offended or threatened her. She was squat as a toad with a long thin nose that sniffed out everybody's business, and keen black eyes that watched people's behavior and understood motives others didn't see.

Bertwoin felt as disappointed as his pigs. Was this his punishment for frustrating them? And speaking of pigs, a shaggy young boar leaned affectionately against Flowia's left leg.

When she saw him, her dark eyes glinted with sudden pleasure. Bertwoin's spirit lifted as if it wanted to wing among the joyful magpies. How could she be so lovely? In her blue dress, she reminded him of the Virgin Mary peering serenely down from the stained-glass window in the abbey's church. How could he have tumbled into such rapture, such luck?

Bertwoin nodded respectfully to the older women as he

strolled toward them. "Good day to you, Na Thea," he said, adding the term of respect.

"And may today's hours be blessed for you, young plowman."

Bertwoin saw the young boar tense as he neared them. He sighed. It seemed he could not be rid of the company of swine this day. It sat on its haunches, eying him as an equal, its face expressionless, its ears pricked erect while it judged his intentions. The pig grunted once as he came even closer—not as a threat, but to mark him as a stranger and therefore maybe not completely welcome.

Then it intensified its gaze, playing the game of who will look away first. Bertwoin did, allowing the boar to win. He then panted at the pig. It acknowledged his greeting with a pant of its own, relaxed, and watched him with the curiosity of one who expects entertainment.

Bertwoin pointed at the porker. "Who's your hairy friend?"

Flowia bent and scratch her fingernails down the brown boar's shaggy back, causing it to smile with porcine contentment.

She chanted

> "This is Roland, my apprentice
> who will hunt forest herbs for me
> with a snuffling snout that cannot miss
> so I may brew everyone's healing tea.
>
> He is also my bodyguard
> armed not with sword or lance
> my knight of the poultry-yard
> bristling with tusks and vigilance."

Na Thea snorted at Flowia's playful description, then

puckered her lips as she considered the boar. "They do train up as well, if not better, than dogs. Knew a farmer who used one to guard his vineyard. Fierce it was. And more loyal than any man." She smirked at Bertwoin, daring him to argue against her.

Bertwoin jerked his head sideways, surrendering to her opinion. Why did Flowia need this boar? Was it because after being captured and almost burned to death, she still had nightmares? Is that why she had decided to train this boar to protect her?

Bertwoin asked Flowia, "You named him Roland?"

"Why shouldn't I?"

He assumed she had named the pig after a long-dead hero killed by the Moors on purpose. It was her way of biting her thumb at people like his uncle who called her a Moor.

"It's just that naming him after a hero shows you expect him to perform great deeds."

Bristling, long-legged, and truffle-nosed, the grunter looked to weigh enough to knock down a full-grown man, even one of his size. Though still young, its curved tusks were long enough to slice open an enemy's belly. Bertwoin kept his movements slow and calm, though he wasn't overly scared of Roland. Most snorters were tolerant and comfortable with people. This one certainly liked Flowia. If only his family, especially his Uncle Laurence, had its good sense.

Flowia picked up a butcher knife and cut off the headless green goose's wings. She then flipped it over on its breast and began ripping large feathers off its back, tossing them into an oak bucket.

"I remember," Na Thea said to Bertwoin, "you once met a boar who wasn't as friendly."

He had met it when he was maybe twelve years old, a half-wild grunter owned by a miserly neighbor. It had attacked his sister, Rachel, while they hunted for honey in the forest.

Luckily for Bertwoin, it wasn't fully grown or experienced, though it had proved to be agile. He had fought and killed the young boar with knife thrusts to its eyes and throat, but not before receiving serious wounds himself. Like his father, Bertwoin's side, chest, and thighs were stitched with scars.

"With your permission," Na Thea said to Flowia, "I'll get on with picking a few herbs out of your back garden."

"Take what you need," Flowia told her.

Bertwoin ached to touch Flowia, to press her warm, firm body against his chest and kiss her and smell the rosemary or lavender rinse she used on her hair. As soon as Na Thea disappeared around the house, she stopped plucking the goose and glided over to him.

He placed his fingertips on her cheek and guided her lips to his. Heat surged into his groin. As they kissed a second time, the pig shoved between them, making them hunch forward to continue their now awkward kiss. Roland pushed his full weight against his rival's shin. Flowia giggled and moved away from Bertwoin.

He said in a voice hoarse with desire, "Your guardian is jealous of me."

"Roland? Bah, you mistake his mood. He sports about half the night with a harem of smitten she-pigs. What you mistake as the glare of envy in his eye is just the shine of indulgent intelligence."

The porker had perked up at the mention of its name and gazed up at her face to see what was wanted of him.

Bertwoin wasn't certain what she meant by indulgent, though he knew the Church sold indulgences to lessen the amount of punishment that sinners had to endure. The idea of Roland as a sinner succored by the Church amused him.

And let people mock Flowia for using uncommon words and for acting better than her birth. Let Abbot Jehan quip that the alchemist might change lead into gold, but he didn't have sufficient magic to turn a prostitute's daughter into a lady. Changing her would ruin her.

"I think," he told her, "that instead of being indulgent, your protector needs to receive an indulgence."

Flowia barked a little laugh, her eyes glinting with merriment.

Bertwoin bent and scratched Roland's bristling back. They might as well be friends, even if they were both vying for the same fair lady. Besides, it was a skirmish Bertwoin expected to win. He could offer more than just loyalty.

Patting the muscular pig, Bertwoin said, "You named him. So he's to be your pet, not your winter meat."

> "He answers to the proud name
> of a hero of yore
> serving me is his aim
> my mighty and formidable boar."

"He'll want a reward. Heroes always expect one." Bertwoin smirked to let her know he was well versed in the ways and manners of heroes.

"And he shall have it." She lifted her hand regally. "Roll over, Roland."

Grunting, the boar rolled onto his back and stretched out full length to expose his belly, smiling with piggy expectation. Flowia squatted beside him and began scratching his belly.

Bertwoin sniffed with disgust at the boar's unabashed display of swinish rapture. "Maybe I should have my belly scratched too?"

Flowia nodded as if this was only to be expected. "I find all males, no matter what animal they represent, are at their core the same." She sucked in her lips, her eyes glinting with devilry. "Since I'm busy with Roland, I will ask Na Thea to scratch your belly for you. She might also delouse you."

Bertwoin resisted an urge to nudge his porcine rival's ribs with his foot. "I think, lady, this sinewy male lying stupefied with pleasure at your feet has taken his reward before it is deserved. What deed has he performed? And do you think you will ever really need his services?"

Flowia rose and glided back to her green goose, disappointing him. "What I think, sir," she said, "is someone's raw jealousy is showing." She began pinching smaller feathers off the limp bird, creating a whirlwind of goose down around the table. Her expression turned serious. "You forget that a murderous monk attacked me here. And monks captured you here. After I train Roland, intruders will have to fight their way into our house. And I saw Tolarto lurking in our woods two days ago. Is he not threat enough to require a champion?"

Bertwoin scowled, his eyes narrowing, and spat. A few months prior, the churlish muleteer had promised to pay him a suckling pig for plowing his fields in spring and then had tried to cheat him out of his fee by claiming he had already made payment when he hadn't. Bertwoin and his father had publicly confronted the rascal in Bourg's weekly market and shamed him into paying his debt. Later, when the abbey's monks had arrested Bertwoin for murder and paraded him through the streets of St. Vincent on their way to the bishop's dungeon, Tolarto had strutted along beside them, mocking Bertwoin.

"Maybe Tolarto needed your help?"

Like Brother Theodoric, the abbey's infirmarian, and Na Thea, Flowia was well-known throughout the *visconte's* domain for being wise in the ways of healing herbs. She dressed wounds, brewed potions, made soothing balms, put together poultices, and otherwise extracted cures from nature's leaves, stems, roots, and flowers. Tolarto claimed to be one of the Good Folk, and they flocked to Flowia since they were banned from visiting the abbey. Brother Theodoric tolerated dissent and never turned away anyone who was sick or wounded, but Abbot Jehan was as unforgiving against heretics as an Old Testament prophet.

"He didn't visit me," she said.

"Why would Tolarto not be afraid of the master?" Bertwoin asked. "Everyone believes the master has magical powers, even if they can't say what they are. Only an idiot would dare steal from the master or otherwise anger him."

Flowia viciously ripped out a handful of down. "Maybe he was just poaching and meant us no real harm. But he is reputed to be a thief, and someone did raid my garden."

"Which one, kitchen or medicine?"

> "My medicinal army of efficacious green
> knights.
> Those bred and grown to fight and conquer
> disease.
> A plant pilferer harvested a company of them
> at night,
> as they waxed under the gibbous moon at their
> ease."

"Why steal from you?" Bertwoin asked. "Anyone needing medicine only has to ask you for it. You are known to be generous even to villains like Tolarto." He waved toward the back of the cottage. "And Na Thea comes to you."

"She has every right to do so. My debt to her can never be repaid. She taught me the secrets of many plants, both those that heal and those that kill."

"Odd, though. Tolarto is more likely to steal wine, coins, or tools than herbs."

Flowia shrugged. "My suspicions still fall upon Tolarto, but I have no proof. The pilferer took pennyroyal and tansy."

Bertwoin hummed. "Two herbs used to end pregnancies. There's a ready market for them."

"Or," Flowia said, "to save his own head."

"Of course, an irate father somewhere." Bertwoin grinned at Roland, who had left him to again sit close to his mistress. "So why did your loyal knight not prevent this crime?"

Flowia gave him a pouty look. "Do not demean my hero. He forages at night and is not yet fully trained. Someday, his ferocity will be legendary."

"He seems well trained for belly scratching."

"Oh well," Flowia said with a mischievous grin, "he's male, and there's pleasure in it. But I'll soon have him trained. Then let the thieves beware. And arrogant monks too. If they ever invade our home again, my shaggy champion will match their cudgels with sinew and tusks. He will scatter them like flapping geese."

Bertwoin glanced at the master's workshop, a separate building similar to the cottage with wattle-and-daub walls and a flat, shingle roof. The monks hunting Bertwoin for Emeline's murder had found him there. Flowia refused to forgive their mean-spirited trespass.

"Is the master in his workshop?" he asked, his voice again husky. When would Na Thea leave?

"No," Flowia said, looking suddenly worried. "He was called to the château before breakfast. Something happened there yesterday, something that angered Sir Jean-Luc."

"So the matter is not trivial," he said.

Visconte Raimon-Rogièr was young, maybe fifteen years old, and so his seneschal and mentor—a battle-hardened cousin—was the most powerful knight in their domain. Sir Jean-Luc kept the accounts, collected taxes, managed the estates, presided over councils, and saw to justice. The *bayles* reported to him.

Na Thea shuffled around the corner of the cottage,

coming from the back garden. "So, Ox," she said with raucous good humor, "are all your chores done so soon?"

"Done? Chores are like hunger, always coming back. There's wheat to thresh, scythes and sickles to sharpen, reeds to be cut for baskets or winnowing sieves, slats on orchard ladders to mend, two mule straps needing repair, and winter wood to gather." He smiled down at Roland. "Then we'll help Perter butcher two pigs for our winter's meat."

"That grunting sinner," said Thea. "He's lucky he still walks above ground instead of sleeping in it."

"What?" Bertwoin asked.

"He was touched by an angel and yet still breathes. Is that not a miracle?" Her sarcasm was as thick as cold porridge.

Flowia and Bertwoin stared at her with their mouths partly open. Na Thea basked in their surprise for a breath or two before adding, "Yea, an angel came down from the heavens and tapped the rascal on his pate. Knocked him to the ground." She cackled. "Lucky for him, his skull makes granite seem soft. Would've been the death of any normal man."

"It's easier to believe a demon thumped him," Bertwoin said. "Why would an angel wing down to visit a heretical pig-sticker?" He frowned when he saw a mischievous glint dawn in Flowia's eyes. "What?" he asked.

She began scraping the goose's pimpled skin with her knife blade to rid it of clinging down. "Was Saint Paul not a greater sinner than Perter?" she asked. "And did not Jesus Himself appear to him and blind him for three days?"

Na Thea rolled her eyes and guffawed. "Yes, think of it? Saint Perter of Carcassonne."

Bertwoin made the sign of the cross over his chest to ward off any possibility of this becoming true, even though the chance of the pig-killer turning into a saint was as remote as finding a single fish in a vast sea.

"Perter a saint," Flowia repeated and shook her head. "Do you think God retains a sense of humor?"

"He does," Bertwoin said with conviction. "Anybody who watches a duck walk knows God likes to laugh."

Na Thea roared again and slapped his shoulder to compliment him.

"Well," Flowia said, her tone prim and serious though her lips trembled as she fought not to smile, "I think Perter wishes to hide the fact that someone bested him in an altercation. Hence we hear this lie about an angel blessing his head. Does a halo now linger over his straw hat?"

Na Thea adjusted spiky burdock in the basket that hung from her bent arm. Bertwoin remembered that burdock was used to treat skin ailments, maybe even leprosy, though he doubted any plant could cure such a dreaded disease.

"Did anyone see this angel, or was Perter the only witness?" he asked.

"Alesta was with him," Na Thea said. "They were coming along the old Roman road when she saw a radiant being wing down and bless the rock Perter calls his head. One thump of the angel's holy forefinger and Perter lay struck down in a trance. The next day, his head throbbed like a beating heart. It shows us that Saint Paul, who was struck down by Christ Himself, must have been a martyr to pain."

So the butcher had suffered like Wilfraed. Good. "Better an angel's divine touch and an aching skull than being stomped on by a ghostly elephant," he joked.

Flowia dismissed this by wiggling three disapproving, goose-blooded fingers near her cheek. "A ghost even of so large a beast could do him no harm. They are of two different worlds. It would step through the solid pig-butcher."

Na Thea scratched her chin. "One of my noble customers saw Domitius pounding along the road three nights ago."

Flowia harrumphed in disbelief. Bertwoin smiled. If her

customers didn't believe in the supernatural, they wouldn't buy holy relics from her.

"Was the angel a man or a woman?" he asked to turn their conversation back to Perter's encounter with the sacred.

Flowia's face hardened. "The Church doesn't allow for female angels."

"Old lechers," he said, "tend to want their beds early when they have young wives. Why were Perter and Alesta out on the road so late at night? He's lucky he didn't meet a roaming demon instead of an angel."

Na Thea squinted at him, her brow furrowed like a badly plowed field. "Returning home from the tavern, why else?"

Bertwoin's heart thumped in his chest. Had he said something wrong?

Flowia's lips twisted into a knowing smile. "Who said the hour was late?"

Bertwoin hesitated a breath too long before saying, "Well, Perter often stays until late at Tisbe's," which was not true. Though the pig-killer carried the burden of many faults, he was not a drunkard. Bertwoin added, "And angels always come in the middle of the night." This was probably also not true.

"Pah!" said Flowia. "I must inform our abbot of a pious plowman who knows the intimate habits of heavenly angels. He'll be amazed. As am I."

"You're as suspicious as a *bayle*," he told her.

Na Thea shook a playful finger at his nose. "I think, Ox, you know more about this attack than *we* do." She gave him a motherly look of pity. "He hit your brother if I remember right. And Clanoud shamed him at a town market for doing so. Was that not enough retribution for you? Or was it Wilfraed who punished the pig-killer?"

"Some punishment," Bertwoin scoffed. "He was visited

and blessed by an angel. Perter is cutting the sweet meat off this bone, not me."

"Little benefit it gave him," Na Thea argued. "He heard no flutter of wings and saw no bright vision of heaven. I doubt he's a better man for it."

Bertwoin asked, "If he was hit by a man or a woman, why would he make up such a story?"

"Because he's as clever as the pigs he butchers," Flowia said, glancing down affectionately at Roland.

"Or maybe the story came not from him," Na Thea said.

Flowia chuckled. "Yes, Alesta is known to be as wily as a Church cardinal. The angel's touch brings her husband respect, while a blow from a man brings him only ridicule."

Na Thea nodded. "And stops the feud between the two households. Now the pig-sticker has no need to get revenge. She's smart if she doesn't tell him what truly happened." The wrinkles around her eyes deepened. "The question is, will others believe Alesta? Rumor has it that the abbot is very interested in knowing more about this angel she saw. It's rumored he intends to question her and test the truth of her words."

Bertwoin fidgeted. "Poor Alesta, he'll twist her up in her lie like a fish caught in a net."

"Ah, so you admit it was a lie," Na Thea said. She looked meaningfully at him. "Liars are often found out."

Bertwoin beamed a sly smile at her. "But as long as the people believe Alesta, there's money to be made from her tale, is there not? Some will believe that angel-struck Perter might be able to pass a bit of his blessing on to them. There might now be a ready market for snips of his hair."

He saw from Flowia's expression that he might have insulted Na Thea.

She laughed. "You're wasted behind a scratch plow, young Bertwoin. If you avoid your father's sins, you'll go far."

"Yes," Flowia muttered, "sins like bashing heads because you overvalue yourself. Because you think revenge is justice. Let's hope the *bayle* doesn't come sniffing around your door." She glanced at the master's workshop where he had been captured by the monks. "Or our door."

"The *bayle* doesn't chase angels."

"No, he chases sinners who walk the Earth. Remember, revenge often turns about and bites the one who grabs its tail."

He bowed slightly to her. "So, now you are a woman wise to the ways of the world."

"You didn't know this?" she asked as if surprised.

"Be careful," Na Thea told Bertwoin, "that those who protect you don't also harm you."

Did she mean that copying his father's pride might harm him, or that Clanoud with his ready fists might do so? "Are you talking of those who fight or those who pray?" he asked to let her know she too should heed her advice.

Na Thea sold religious relics and cures to noblewomen and noblemen—those who fought—but she often criticized their arrogance. She also had the habit of making offerings to pagan spirits, though she took communion from those who prayed. She worried little about offending the people who protected her.

"Both, Ox," she said, not pleased with his hinting at her hypocrisy. "And…" She stared at a boy of about ten who had just trotted through the mulberry hedge's opening.

The boy marched up to Flowia and said, "The master says you are to fetch the plowman," he glanced at Bertwoin, "and bring him to the château at once."

CHAPTER V.

After the boy had trotted away, Na Thea crowed, "Well, Flowia, it seems today you're blessed with better luck than the Magi had. The master tells you to fetch Ox, and you don't even have to shift yourself because what you seek stands at your very door." She scratched her cheek and smirked at Bertwoin. "Though I think this plowman often brings himself to your door."

She raised her basket full of cut herbs and plants for them to see. "I thank you for these, Flowia." She nodded to them and marched away.

Flowia tore out a last handful of feathers and inspected the headless green goose. "I'll singe the stubble off later. So, I am to take you to the château. Good. I need to bring Hytha a beauty potion anyway. Let me fetch it."

"I hope I'm not being called there to answer for Perter's headache," he muttered. "Oh, you don't think he died, do you?"

Flowia stepped close to him and put a finger over his lips to silence his doubts. "If so, do you think the master would summon you to the château? Or would warn you to flee to the mountains?"

Bertwoin blew out his breath. "You're right. But I hope it's not another killing."

The master had a reputation for solving murders, which was the reason Bertwoin had run to him when he was accused of killing the woodcutter's daughter. At that time, he had believed, as nearly everyone else did, that the alchemist used magic to ferret out the names of guilty criminals.

Flowia left the bucket full of white and gray feathers where it stood and carried the naked goose into the cottage. Roland trotted in after her, but she pointed at the doorway and ordered the pig back outside. Roland sat down and looked up at her, his eyes pleading. She nudged him with her foot until with great reluctance he exited.

So Bertwoin waited in the poultry yard with Flowia's other hairy guardian. Roland sat on his hams, relaxed with a piggy smile under his snout. A bee buzzed near his head, and he snapped at it as a dog would, then looked surprisingly philosophical when he missed. Ignoring Bertwoin, Roland stared at the cottage's open doorway as if waiting for the return of the goddess he worshipped.

Bertwoin understood the boar's fondness for Flowia, though he hoped she didn't become overly tolerant toward the beast. An annoyingly attentive pig might hinder his lovemaking.

He told the boar, "I wish I was as relaxed as you."

Roland tilted his hairy head and stared up into Bertwoin's face, his eyes alert and curious. It was difficult to dislike a beast that seemed so eager to please.

Flowia flounced through the doorway, carrying her wooden sabots and a fist-sized flap of leather wrapped around something, probably a glass vial or tiny clay pot filled with the beauty lotion she had mentioned.

She had changed her brown apron for an unbloodied, white one. Her thick hair was now tucked up into a white linen coif under a woven hemp hat, the coif's white chin-band framing the lower half of her face.

"Do you make beauty lotions for yourself too?" he asked.

"Why? Do I need to?"

"If you do, they are working."

Her skin, smooth as hazelnut paste, along with her delicate features made his breath catch in his throat every time he saw her anew. If only he could convince his family that her dark beauty, her clever brain, and the few sheep she owned were enough of a dowry to overcome the fact that she had no father and people said her mother had been a whore?

Roland pranced over to her, as did Bertwoin.

Without a word, Flowia glided out through the opening in the mulberry hedge with Bertwoin toward the château. When she saw Roland trotting along behind them, Flowia pointed at the workshop and ordered him to stay, an order he ignored, though he did wince with disappointment.

So they marched on, with Roland grunting along behind them.

Bertwoin chuckled. Yes, her husband would have to take care and fight to have his say in things if he wanted to be more than just her servant. Of course, Roland probably would protect her garden and Flowia too because it was in its interest to do so. She fed him. And he would roll over to have his hairy belly scratched. Who wouldn't? But swine also rebelled and did as *they* wished, as Roland was doing even now.

Along the way, Roland became distracted by a sow in the woods and trotted off to investigate possibilities.

Flowia stayed quiet as they strode along the bank of the murmuring Aude River with wisps of morning mist sliding over its smooth, green surface. Nipping mosquitoes still lay abed.

They were crossing the wooden bridge when they spied the master marching toward them in his usual ankle-length red robe with a red cap covering his white hair. His facial muscles drooped with either fatigue or worry until he noticed them and smiled, dropping years off his face.

"Well met," he cried. "I thought I would pass the time waiting here on the bridge for you come. You have outrun my expectation."

"He was visiting our house," Flowia explained.

"You didn't send the boy to fetch me at my house," Bertwoin said.

"I feared your father might prevent your coming. I also knew Flowia would find you, wherever you were hiding."

So the master knew he had been hiding in the woods. Did everyone know this?

"Is all well with you?" Flowia asked.

"Yes, daughter, but all is not well at the château, and since the walls there seemed to have eyes and ears, I wanted us to talk here in private." The master glanced at the walled citadel, which sprawled across the top of a flat hill. The length of its wall and the height of its clustered towers would make any emperor lust to own it. Three towns, two walled and one not, lay curled around the hill's bottom.

"Have you heard that Perter was touched by an angel?" Bertwoin asked. He hoped to hear that the pig-butcher had nothing to do with his going to the château.

The master chuckled. "Ah yes, I was told the tale. He works in the château's forecourt even now and sports a great bandage under his hat. Some mock him for it. Others treat him as though he now wears a heavenly crown."

Bertwoin studied the alchemist, trying to determine his

feelings on the matter. He saw no sign of scorn or of its opposite feeling, respect. "What do you think of his story, master?"

"Ah well, I think those who pray do not like miracles happening outside of their control. But doubting monks and clerics have to be careful lest they disclaim a divine visitation that was truly sacred." He rolled his eyes. "I doubt the churlish butcher had a St. Paul moment on the road. And I also doubt it was a thief. Alesta would never scare away a ruffian intent on robbery."

Flowia eyed Bertwoin and smiled.

> "But not all ruffians are thieves.
> Some think themselves knights
> with a cause up their sleeves
> and revenge as their right."

The alchemist gave Bertwoin a knowing look. "I thought your father had already salved your family's honor."

Bertwoin sighed. Could everyone see his sins so easily? "Is this another murder?" he asked.

"Sir Jean-Luc has tasked me with the duty of determining that very question. I have profitable work for you, plowman, if you are quick on your feet, keep wit in your head, and wield a polite tongue."

Pretending to be surprised anyone might think otherwise, Bertwoin tapped his chest. "How else would you describe me?"

When Flowia snorted, he appealed to her with his hands outstretched in front of him, his palms up. "What part of the description doesn't suit me?"

"You will work at the château," the alchemist said.

"What? The château?" He would be trapped inside the high walls with the stout pig-butcher. Perter was familiar with the château, its dark corners and puzzling routines, and would have the advantage over him. "I have bucketfuls of work to do at home. My father will forbid me to go. He'll not let me leave my chores at the farm undone."

The alchemist waved a hand as if flicking aside an annoying gnat. "The seneschal has already agreed to this. If Clanoud objects, he can argue with Sir Jean-Luc."

The master cleared his throat. "A bellows worker in the château's kitchen fell to the floor and died after a fit of convulsions. Not long before this, Arundel had boxed his ear."

"Do you think the chef struck him too hard?" Flowia asked.

"It's possible, but Arundel has ten years of experience at boxing ears. I doubt he caused the boy's death."

"Could it not be a natural death from sickness?" Bertwoin asked, hoping to raise an argument that would change the master's mind and save him being sent into the lion's den.

The alchemist sucked in his cheeks and shook his head. "Arundel would never allow a sick person to enter his kitchen. He is also holding something back, as are all those who work for him. I see it in their manner and feel it in my blood. There is something sinister in this death."

Bertwoin felt himself becoming entangled like a fish in a net. "Does that not argue for the idea that Arundel caused the boy's death? That he lost control this time and hit him too hard?"

"When I asked him why he had hit the boy, Arundel said it was a trifling matter. The boy was poaching food meant for his betters. But I felt angry fear in Arundel. It filled the kitchen like the fume of burnt meat. And while we spoke, no one toiling in the kitchen looked eye-to-eye at us. They pretended I wasn't there, and that they weren't listening to us. If all were honest in that kitchen, they would have watched us with an open countenance and frank interest."

Relenting to the master's will, Bertwoin asked, "What am I to do at the château?"

"Ah well, I think we should place you in the kitchen."

"I'll not let Arundel box my ears."

"You fear it was poison?" Flowia asked the master.

"I do. And I fear it was destined for the high table."

Bertwoin was shocked. "What? Am I to work then as a taster?"

Giggling, Flowia slapped his forearm. "Hah! What would kill *Visconte* Raimon-Rogièr or *Viscontesse* Agnes wouldn't even upset your lowborn stomach."

The master chuckled. "No, plowman, you will watch and listen. You will ask astute questions under the table."

"And you think they will talk to me?"

"More so than to me. You *are* a local hero, are you not? You tweaked the bishop's noble nose by escaping from his dungeon and still walk free."

"Me? It was Flowia who spirited me out of prison."

And," the alchemist said, smiling like a fox eying an unwary mouse, "does Eudes not work there?"

"He does," Bertwoin admitted grumpily. Eudes was a young grill cook who courted his sister, Rachel. He would want to gain and keep the good opinion of everyone in her family.

The master snapped his fingers. "Then off you go. I need not return to the château. All is arranged for you to work in the kitchen. The château's steward will have his orders by now. See him and not Arundel. The chef will balk at letting you work in his kitchen."

The master threw Flowia a sidelong glance. "On second thought, the steward is a haughty fellow too and will not like obeying an order he knows originated with me. He might avoid meeting with you." The old man nodded at the flap of leather in her hand. "Who is that is for?"

"Hytha."

"Good. He will not disobey her. She has the ear of the *viscontesse*. Try to persuade her to find the steward and tell him to meet you." He patted her shoulder. "And you also have your ways of gleaning what we need to know. The maids-in-waiting and servants will talk to you. And both of you will fare better if not seen in my company. God keep you in His hand."

CHAPTER VI.

Flowia and Bertwoin marched into clamorous Castellar, one of the three towns sprawling along the base of the citadel's broad hill. She then led him through the section given over to those who wielded hammers, mainly carpenters and one blacksmith they heard banging an anvil in his open-sided workshop. It was not yet the wet times, so the lanes were dusty instead of sticky with sucking mud. She stopped to slip on her sabots.

Many of the people they met nodded and stared at them with naked curiosity. That was to be expected. The alchemist's virgin coming to their town probably meant she was on an errand for the master. And she carried something mysterious wrapped in a scrap of leather. Did that mean someone was sick at the château? If so, why did she need a plowman's help.

A mongrel with a bleeding slash on its snout lay against a wall, chewing on a gray rat. Bertwoin assumed the dead rat had gotten in one telling bite before it became the dog's meal. It was good to leave one's mark.

Watching the mutt gnaw on the rat made him think of

the château's kitchen. What kind of work could he do there other than the hot, red-faced work of a bellows boy?

"How am I ever going to pry clues out of Arundel?" he asked.

"Use your wit, something you are known to possess."

"He'll be no more prone to talk to me than the Pope. I'm a nobody to him and won't be welcome in his kitchen." Bertwoin leaned forward as he and Flowia left Castellar's highest houses behind them and began to trudge up the grassy slope toward Carcassonne's formidable wall and impassive towers.

"Maybe," Flowia said. "But the master's word carries weight with both Sir Jean-Luc and *Visconte* Raimon-Rogièr, and you will be there at his behest. That gives you a modicum of status. Besides, Arundel should think it in his best interest to lend you his support. If you assist the master in proving that someone sabotaged his kitchen, then any doubts anyone has about his cooking killing anyone will be disclaimed."

Bertwoin laughed. "Yes, *disclaimed*. Maybe you should come and argue for me, maiden."

"I would be more successful arguing against the wind. Arundel fears me."

"Arundel? The kitchen tyrant? Why would he ever be scared of you?"

"It's a secret he and I keep between us. In fact, what he fears is my *not* keeping his secret."

Bertwoin expected her to know many things people kept hidden from others. As a healer and one who kept an ear turned toward the local gossip, she heard whispers and secrets. It gave her a certain power.

The guard slouching at the Narbonne Gate's barbican was chatting with a silk merchant and ignored them and all other visitors, many who carried sacks of grain or produce or live chickens into the citadel. Flowia and Bertwoin hurried through the narrow streets to the barbican of Château

Comtal and crossed its stone bridge over a dry moat. A tall soldier standing guard at the eastern gate between two towers with blue-tiled roofs stared off as if in a trance and, like the sentry at the citadel's barbican, ignored them.

Flowia glanced at him. "Maybe they fight better than they keep watch."

"Well," he grumbled, "they don't have to keep a lookout for me, do they?"

"If the master needs you in the kitchen," Flowia said in the tone of a mother admonishing her son, "you will be put to work there. Sir Jean-Luc agreed to this and will keep his *bayle* on a leash." Her smile turned playful. "But it might be wise not to show Perter your back while he's holding a butcher knife."

Bertwoin grinned. "If the pig-sticker comes for me, I'll just ring his bell again."

She poked his ribs with a forefinger. "Don't puff up too much. And don't embarrass the master. You carry the weight of his official recommendation on your crooked shoulders."

"Well, let's hope it doesn't slide from my left shoulder across the back of my neck and fall off my right one," he said, referring to the fact that like most plowman, his left shoulder was higher than his right.

"It's an honorable mark of your trade," she said.

Servants bustled about as they prepared to honor the seneschal's son, Master Servay, on his name day. Not far from a forge set up in the middle of the château's forecourt shaded by elm trees, Perter butchered a sow hung up by its hind legs on a wooden frame. He wore a wad of hemp cloth under his straw hat. Blood flowed down his wrists and bare forearms and dripped from his elbows. Two dirty children in patched tunics watched him like mongrels hoping for meat scraps.

Bertwoin groaned inwardly. He would have to stay as alert as a stag that hears the yowling of eager greyhounds. Even being tucked inside Arundel's kitchen might not be far enough away from the ill-tempered butcher. The rascal was sure to insult him and to try to trip him or otherwise embarrass him.

Flowia stopped a bowman as he walked past them and told him Hytha wanted to see them. He nodded, signed for them to wait, and hurried into a narrow passageway leading to the Aude Gate.

"Do not be willful when she comes," Flowia ordered.

Bertwoin folded his hands across his stomach in the manner of a humble monk and intoned, "That's interesting advice coming from you, maiden." He was not going to roll over on command as Roland had done...at least, not always. He dropped the monkish manner and said in his normal tone, "Your saying that is like a hen telling a rooster to stop acting like a chicken."

She smiled as if he had complimented her, which irritated him. He often couldn't predict her reactions. She sometimes took insult at an innocent comment he made, yet at other times laughed as if he were joking when he was serious.

He turned to watch Perter slice meat off the gutted pig. The man had skill. The stink of fresh blood hung thick in the forecourt's air. A bird in one of the elm trees fussed at something. Bertwoin knew how it felt.

Hytha, a maid-in-waiting to *Viscontesse* Agnes, strode out of a cellar door followed by the bowman who had fetched her. He pointed to them, then ducked back inside the cellar. Hytha swept toward them with dignity, stopped in front of them, and waited in regal silence.

After greeting her, Flowia asked if she had seen the master.

"Aye, I have. He examined the dead boy's body before it was carried away." Hytha's lips twisted to one side. "Perhaps he will burn sage or mint or sweet fennel in his workshop this night and raise the killer's visage in the smoke. That is, if the boy *was* poisoned as he believes. Then perhaps we may persuade him to use his special skills to putrefy the killer's organs and slowly punish the man for us."

Bertwoin itched to point out that the killer, if there was one, might instead be female. Poison was often a woman's weapon. But he thought it wiser to keep quiet. He wasn't certain whether Hytha was ridiculing people's belief in the alchemist's abilities or if she really believed the master could ferret out the murderer by performing magic. It pleased him that even in the château, no one truly knew what powers the master owned.

Flowia, clearly irked to hear anyone, even a maid-in-waiting joke about her master, said, "We use our sage and fennel to fit other purposes. And the master has experience solving murders."

She unwrapped the flap of leather to reveal a small glass vial and handed it to Hytha, who held the reddish lotion up to the sunlight as if to judge its potency. She nodded, then reached into a pocket hidden in her robe and pulled out two silver deniers for Flowia.

Beauty potions pay better than medicines, Bertwoin thought. The healing salves his *maman* made and sold fetched only vegetables or other bartered goods as payment.

Flowia nodded at Bertwoin. "This is the one the master told Sir Jean-Luc about."

Hytha looked Bertwoin over as though he, like the lotion, were for sale. "So this is the one people call Ox? He's big enough. Is he clumsy?"

Flowia laughed. "Only when he tries to make speeches. He can fetch with the best of them and is strong enough to lift a cask."

When both Hytha and Bertwoin looked at her in surprise,

she added, "An empty one, of course." She smiled. "But his head is not empty. He's as smart as any wild pig."

Bertwoin said nothing so as not to make a mistake and prove Flowia right about his clumsy speech. He chuckled inwardly at her selling of him. She had no idea whether he could lift a cask, empty or not. And an ox that was as smart as a boar would be a valuable animal.

Hytha glanced from him to Flowia and back again as if judging how well the master's virgin liked this plowman. Then she smirked. "Can he carry a drunken man to bed?"

Flowia chucked her tongue. "As long as it's not himself." They both laughed.

Hytha said, "Wait here. I'll find the steward. He's been told to settle the plowman in the kitchen. Arundel might resist a little but he'll do as he's told."

She smiled a little to herself as if putting Bertwoin in Arundel's kitchen amused her, then swished away toward the far end of the forecourt. Flowia told Bertwoin to behave and keep his opinions to himself while he was within the château walls.

He folded his arms over his chest. "You, of course, would do that. I have enough work at home and in the fields."

"Watch those around you," Flowia continued as if deaf to his complaints. "You'll need the alert eyes and ears of a falcon if you are to answer the master's questions." She elbowed his ribs. "And stop looking as recalcitrant as an overloaded mule. There's solid coin to be had for carrying firewood or washing the château's dishes. Your father will be well pleased."

Bertwoin pointed at a man in leather breeches and a tight tunic who carried a mallet and chisel toward a tower where the roof was being repaired. "I'm as out of place here as I would be drinking with masons in their lodge. This château is full of secrets and habits I do not know. Cutting furrows in open fields is the work I am trained to do."

"Then you'll need to learn the château's noble ways quickly. The master wants you here. And if you despise having deniers, give them to your parents. They are sure to welcome the money, as will Rachel. The heavier her dowry, the more handsome her husband will be."

The steward stalked along with the measured gait of a hunting heron. Bertwoin prepared for an officious meeting. The man's mantle was trimmed in squirrel fur, and he carried a stick of ash decorated with filigreed silver.

Like Hytha had done, he too stopped and waited without greeting them.

Flowia curtsied. "The master alchemist thought there might be work for the plowman in the château's kitchen."

"So I was told. This is Clanoud's son?"

"I am," Bertwoin said before Flowia could answer for him. He was beginning to feel like a ram under discussion for stud duty.

"Your father is a good farmer," the steward told Bertwoin. "Always pays his taxes and rents on time. We can use you for day work. Go help Perter the Touched with his butchering." He saw Bertwoin's surprise and dismay. "You have a problem working with the pig-killer?"

Bertwoin had expected to replace the dead bellows boy. He would do the alchemist little good if the steward stranded him in the forecourt.

"The master wanted me in the kitchen."

"The alchemist's desires hold little sway here, peasant. The seneschal didn't tell me you had to be *inside* the kitchen. Assisting Perter with butchering swine helps Arundel."

Bertwoin shrugged. The master would not thank him if he argued with the steward and was sent back home. "Well, I know how to get along with the pig-butcher."

"Good," the steward said, his tone condescending. "Many don't." He glanced at Perter, and his lip curled. "Which might be why today he wears a dressing cloth under his hat. And don't think he's a saint now that he says an angel blessed his pate. Work well and cause no problems, plowman, if you want to remain within these walls."

A carter beside a two-wheeled wagon loaded with wine barrels called to the steward, who yelled back, "Do you still not know where to store your wine?" and hurried away.

"So I am to work outside the kitchen," Bertwoin muttered.

"Only for a short while if the master wishes otherwise." Flowia countered his surly manner with a smile as sweet as ripe berries and squeezed his hand. "Just remember that people find willing backs easy to use."

She stared a moment at Perter's back and watched him slice meat off the sow's carcass. "It would please me much to stay and watch you and the blessed butcher toil together, but I have one or two women to visit as the master asked."

"Do you not think it a joke that the pig-sticker is now called the Touched?" he asked.

"I think that if you acting less like your father, he would not be called that."

Bertwoin became all attention when he saw his other enemy, Tolarto Malet, carry a canvas sack to the kitchen door. "There goes a second knave whose company brings me no joy."

Flowia turned and hummed agreement. "Another scoundrel who might slide a knife in your back. It's strange to see him here. I would not expect Tolarto to think kindly of the *visconte* or his seneschal."

"Just the opposite, in fact," Bertwoin said.

One of Tolarto's brothers had been caught poaching deer in the forest. After the young *visconte* had punished the thief -on Jean-Luc's insistence—by having his hand chopped off, the wrist wound had festered, and Tolarto's brother had suffered a feverish death.

"Tolarto never threatens the *visconte* or his seneschal out loud, but he makes it known he believes only weak men forgive others. Yet they let him come and go as he pleases."

Flowia waved at the people hustling about in the fore-court. "Who doesn't come here? And he *is* a carter. Still, it would be interesting to know if *he* was here yesterday."

Bertwoin grunted. His working for the château might well be worth his time if it led to his catching Tolarto as a murderer. He needed to talk with Eudes.

Flowia lifted the front of her dress off the ground. "Don't make yourself the leper at the feast, dearest plowman."

"When will I see you again?"

"When coins clink in your fist, of course" she teased.

"Will I get paid today?" He saw that his wanting to be with her pleased her.

She gave him a little catlike smile. "No, but you will visit the master tonight to tell him what you learned. You may see me then."

"Alone?"

"Perhaps we can walk awhile." She turned and glided away toward the East Gate.

"Walking wasn't my hope," he called to her back.

She raised a hand above her left shoulder and wiggled her fingers, saying goodbye without looking back at him. From her posture, he guessed that she was smiling.

CHAPTER VII.

Bertwoin strolled over to where Perter sat on a stool and watched him carve a pork loin off the hanging sow. The butcher's movements resembled a dance, practiced and pleasing, ritualistic and magical.

"What do you want, slump-shoulder?" Perter snarled.

"I was told I had to work with you."

"You?" For half a breath, the pig-bleeder's face creased with worry. "Well, well. So you can do more than just push a plow and sniff mule farts all day, eh? I thought you'd be too proud to carve meat."

"Mule farts smell like perfume compared to the stink of your crotch, pig-sticker. Flies drop from the air when they enter the fume of your reek."

Perter pointed his knife blade at Bertwoin's belly. "If I have to get up from here, you'll be the vermin that drops."

"Come for me and I'll finish what the demon didn't. Then the flies will feast."

Perter grunted. "It was an angel, mule-fart, an angel fresh from heaven. Alesta saw it swoop down to me as clear as a bright star. Such a thing will never happen to the likes of you." He glanced around the crowded courtyard. "Or anyone else here."

"If that's the way of a blessing, I'll forgo it. And if it was an angel, it wasn't sent to honor you but to punish you for some raw sin."

"I sin no worse than any other man," Perter said and turned back to slicing meat.

Bertwoin relaxed. So Alesta hadn't told the pig-killer who had hit him. If she had, they would already be brawling. Maybe he didn't have to watch his back around the butcher as closely as he thought.

He told Perter, "The steward says we are to work together."

"Why come here to drudge for *Visconte* Raimon-Rogièr?" the pig-killer asked. "Why not work for the abbey? Monks and clerics take joy in punishing themselves. They like being punched in the face. Working with you would take the place of flagellation."

The butcher was chiding him about the night he had sneaked the alchemist into the abbey to secretly examine Emeline's corpse. An uncommonly fast monk, a greyhound in a black robe, had spied him, given chase, and run him down. But catching an intruder was not the same as vanquishing him. Bertwoin had smacked the brother on the nose.

He folded his arms over his chest. "I'm willing to work or to watch you work. Whichever way you want it."

Perter grunted and waved a bloody hand in the kitchen's direction. "Go bother someone else. Arundel is short a bellows boy. Even a one-trick dog like you can keep a fire hot."

"I don't want to end up dead like that boy. Some say he took someone else's death."

Perter swallowed before saying, "A poisoner? Women's gossip. He just got a good taste of that swill Arundel serves.

Snatched up a bite of tainted food, and it dropped him like hemlock does a pig. Or just as likely, he wasn't poisoned at all. The chef just hit him too hard when he caught him thieving. Arundel has a temper on him like a boar with a sour belly."

"So the boy didn't have any serious enemies?"

"Nah." Perter glanced up at the elms shading him, remembering something. "Though I heard Tolarto kicked him about some. Said the boy had stolen from him." He grunted. "Nothing inflames a thief more than to have another thief steal from him."

"That's heavy punishment for a little thieving."

"Unless the boy didn't stop."

Bertwoin felt a prickle of excitement. "I did see Tolarto enter the kitchen as if he belonged there."

The pig-man grunted again. "If it was a poisoning done on purpose and the boy ate it by accident, Tolarto would be the man to look at. He hates the *visconte* worse than the pox."

Now Bertwoin had something to tell the alchemist. He looked around. The steward wouldn't be pleased if he found him standing by and not working, so he reminded Perter, "I can stay here and just bathe in the halo of your blessed presence or I can work."

"You know how to butcher?"

"I've helped lay in our winter meat."

Perter stabbed the long knife between two ribs in the hanging carcass and left it sticking there. "Finish cutting meat off this one then, left side only, not the royal side. I need to ready a second pig."

Bertwoin began slicing flesh off the gutted sow while armies of flying insects besieged the carcass and his sweaty face. Perter disappeared. Bertwoin glanced around and didn't see anyone of authority. He cut off a hunk of fatty meat and tossed it to the two half-starved boys still waiting for a handout.

"Go on, now," he ordered. "And don't let the steward see you."

They ran off with their treasure before Perter caught him "stealing" food and giving it away.

The pig-killer dragged a squealing porker by its hind legs into the forecourt. A boy followed him, carrying a bucket.

Under the elms, Perter straddled the struggling pig, trapping it between his sturdy legs. He bent over it, panted into its face to relax it, then whispered into its right ear until it calmed. Cooing to it, he scratched its bristly neck. Then he shoved its head forward and slit its throat almost as if he were caressing it. The boy slipped his bucket under the screaming, shuddering pig and caught the spurting blood so Arundel could use it to make black sausage.

Perter saw Bertwoin watching him. "What're you gawking at? Ain't you paid to work like everyone else?"

"I didn't know anyone paid you for this. I thought you owed it to the *visconte*."

Perter's face tightened with sudden hatred, and his lips clamped together. Bertwoin knew he was here because he owed the *visconte* a number of days of labor. And like Tolarto, the pig-killer probably had little liking for those who lived in the château. Sir Jean-Luc had taken Perter's mother-in-law, Éléonore Faure, as his mistress and then had cast her aside when he had tired of her.

The butcher looked ready to straddle Bertwoin's back and slit his peasant throat. "So you think you're better than me, eh?"

"You're the one with the big head this morning, not me. I owe the *visconte* work days too." The butcher didn't need to know this wasn't one of them.

Perter grunted. "It's a debt I willingly pay. I've got no quarrel with our *visconte*." He watched the dying pig's final throes. "So why do you plague us here inside the château?

You're a plow pusher. Why not pay off your work debt doing what you know how to do?"

"I like to learn new skills. Just watching a master like you among the hogs will make me a better butcher."

"Don't mock me, mule's ass." Perter's scowl would have frightened off a bear. "Your pa should've taught you some manners."

"I just don't like listening to your blather. Maybe another demon needs to visit you to improve your temper."

"The devil take you, fart-sniffer." Perter stepped closer to Bertwoin and grabbed the long knife out of his hand. He then began hacking chunks of bloody pork off the hanging carcass. "I'll cut and you carry. And take your time. That way, I won't have to see so much of your blasted face."

Bertwoin smiled at the butcher's back. Now he had a reason to be the kitchen.

CHAPTER VIII.

Bertwoin lugged a blood-slicked ham to the kitchen for Perter and stood just inside the doorway, scanning the room. It was unusually quiet. A tense trio—Hytha the maid-in-waiting, a haughty knight named Sir Philippe de Nimes, and a knight-hostage named Sir Reginald de Lastours—clustered near the doorway of the larder. Why would they be in the kitchen?

Eudes caught Bertwoin's eye and pointed with a pair of tongs at a massive table. Bertwoin nodded thanks, entered, and dropped the meat on it. He needed to talk with Eudes, who had witnessed the bellows boy's death, but the cook was busy at the moment. He expected Eudes to be helpful because he wanted to please everyone in Rachel's family while they were deciding on whom she should marry.

Now that Bertwoin was inside the kitchen, he could tell that the nobles were arguing. Hytha's face was pale and tight with righteous anger. Everyone in the kitchen was careful to stay as quiet as rabbits so they could listen to the argument.

"You presume too much, sir" Hytha hissed at Sir Reginald.

"I never presume," Reginald de Lastours said, his tone a

lazy drawl of studied boredom. "Saying I presume too much is presumptuous. Your own words argue against you."

"Then you have misinterpreted my words, sir."

"But I trust words to mean exactly what they say. It's a fault of mine to be so trusting. Do I not trust my father's word that he'll not do that which will anger *Visconte* Raimon-Rogièr or Sir Jean-Luc and get me hanged?"

"But it is your father's acts that will get you hanged, not his words," argued Sir Philippe de Nimes with the glee of someone tossing a higher score at dice. "And you are a hostage here because the *visconte* does not trust your father's words to mean exactly what he will do."

Sir Reginald touched his forehead and waved his hand at Sir Philippe to show he admired his opponent's reasoning. "Like young *Visconte* Raimon-Rogièr, our maid-in-waiting here is replete with sad mistrust."

Hytha thrust her head toward Sir Reginald with hen-like anger. "If we cannot trust the father, why should we believe the son? A cherry tree begets cherries. You should learn your place here, I think. Else my mistress will have you whipped."

Sir Reginald's eyes widened in delight. "And I think you presume too much when you begin to speak for your mistress."

It was well known that both Sir Reginald and Sir Philippe were attentive to young *Viscontesse* Agnes, and so, both were often in her company.

Sir Philippe's nostrils flared as he raised a menacing fist between their chests. "I will not have you insult a lady."

Sir Reginald yawned. "In this region, 'lady' is a title often bestowed upon those who disprove the honorific given them. It shows a certain laxity towards the truth and degrades the title itself." Reginald's smirk dared Sir Philippe to strike him. "I've even heard a man address a horse, a pretty hunter I will admit, as Lady."

Both men were in their early twenties, of equal height, and were muscular enough to be both agile and strong. Bertwoin wondered who would win their kitchen brawl if it came to that. Would they draw their daggers?

"And as for the 'gentlemen' around here," Sir Reginald continued, "barbarians, even when dressed in fine clothes, still wipe their fingers in their beards to clean off the grease."

The best dressed person in the kitchen, of course, was the hostage-knight. He wore pointed shoes and red-and-white striped hose under a knee-length black tunic, the most expensive dye for cloth. Bertwoin had heard that wherever Sir Reginald went, whether riding a palfrey through the forest or feasting in the great hall, he strove to dress well and be noticed.

"You call us dirty barbarians?" Hytha muttered. "I'll wager this kitchen is as clean as the one in your father's grand château."

With bored disdain, Sir Reginald drawled, "My father's chef doesn't make it a habit of leaving dead boys lying about in his kitchen."

Arundel's meat cleaver chopped a pork loin with ringing force, startling everyone.

Sir Philippe rolled his eyes. "Calling a single tragedy a habit misconstrues the truth." He added with languid nonchalance, "I say *tragedy* but that is not quite accurate, is it? Had one of the *visconte's* favorite mastiffs died, that would have been a true tragedy."

Sir Reginald smiled at Hytha. "Tragedy enough for the *viscontesse* to send her maid-in-waiting to inspect the kitchen."

"My lady wishes to be apprised of the situation."

"And you, sir," Sir Philippe said, "why do you invade the chef's kitchen?"

"Because, sir, I am hungry and in need of a bit of sustenance."

"You do not have your squire fetch food for you?"

Sir Reginald smirked at Arundel. "The chef delays when serving my squire yet does not do so with me." He turned to Hytha. "And pray tell, what will you tell your mistress about-"

"Why are you standing about?" someone complained. Bertwoin turned to see Perter staring at him. "Must I do everything?"

"You," Sir Philippe called to Bertwoin, clearly welcoming the opportunity to escape from the hostilities swelling between himself and Sir Reginald. "What are you staring at, peasant?"

Bertwoin saw Eudes shake his head to warn him not to provoke this knight's anger. But by calling him a peasant, though he was one, Sir Philippe meant to insult him.

"Nothing," he told the arrogant warrior. "I'm just a lowly servant carrying raw meat into the kitchen so the barbarians may grease their beards."

Reginald, who unlike most knights was clean-shaven, hawed and grinned at Bertwoin. "Well, well. A château servant who truly judges the manners of this locale. And pray tell me, fellow, since your beard seems clean, what do you wipe your greasy fingers on when at table?"

"Why, sir," Bertwoin said, adopting Sir Reginald's dignified drone, "I use a little silk napkin, of course."

Both Hytha and Sir Reginald and everyone else in the kitchen except Sir Philippe laughed at the ridiculous idea of him owning so expensive a napkin...or using one.

"Get on with your work, knave," Sir Philippe growled at Bertwoin through clenched teeth. "Or I'll have you whipped for insolence." He studied Bertwoin, as if memorizing his face. "How are you called?"

"I'm nobody whose name is worth the breath of a nobleman. People call me Ox." Bertwoin bowed. "With your permission." He turned and shoved past the pig-killer, retreating before Sir Philippe could confront him further.

Glancing back, he saw Sir Reginald laughing and Hytha with a slender hand over her mouth to hide a smile. Perter grinned at him, probably delighted that Sir Philippe was displeased with him. He must avoid this knight whenever possible.

As Bertwoin hurried toward the butchering rack, the *bayle* saw him and strolled over, shaking his head. "So the old devil sent you here to spy on us, heh? He thinks it was murder."

"Whatever do you mean?" Bertwoin asked as if surprised anyone would think the alchemist had sent him to the château.

The *bayle* pursed his lips. "I'll admit that murder is a possibility. And the old pinch-fist *is right* more often than not."

"If it wasn't murder, the master will prove that also."

"Humm. An accident would also fall to my favor." The lawman straightened to full height. "I'll want to be kept informed if you learn anything."

"Of course."

The *bayle* looked unconvinced, but he brushed past him and strolled toward the kitchen.

Perter strutted out into the courtyard and tilted his head back to let the sun warm his face. He then swaggered over to Bertwoin and said, "You'd best carry in the rest of the hog and be quick about it. You'll not be working long for me."

"*With* you, not *for* you," Bertwoin said.

Perter grunted, his eyes glowing with satisfaction. "Sir Philippe intends to complain to the château steward about you. Maybe they'll rip out a tooth or two to teach you to keep your saucy mouth shut."

"I gave him due respect," Bertwoin said. He waved at the hanging carcass. "Cut it and I'll carry it, pig-bleeder."

Eudes poked his nose out of the kitchen's arched doorway like a rabbit about to leave its warren, then strode toward the passageway leading to the château's main food cellar. Bertwoin hastened to follow him.

"Heh, where do you think you're going, mule-fart?" Perter called to Bertwoin's back.

"To pee. I don't just let it run down my leg like you do."

CHAPTER IX

Bertwoin made sure the pig-sticker didn't see him dodge inside the cellar. Leaving the door open to give himself enough light, he skipped down a steep flight of stone steps that probably earned a curse from every carter carrying a load.

Eudes waited for him in the cellar. The cavernous room spread out darkly around them, its ceiling low, the musty odor of its damp earthen floor reminding Bertwoin of the early mornings when he plowed fields glazed with dew. Someone rumbled about near a back wall, moving barrels, but Bertwoin judged the person was too far away to hear them if they kept their voices low.

"Watch your step with Sir Philippe," Eudes whispered. "He takes pleasure in punishing servants and peasants. It's sport to him."

"Was I so disrespectful?"

"You made Sir Reginald laugh against us. That's offense enough. After you left, Sir Philippe told the maid-in-waiting he intends to have you put on latrine duty. I've seen him do likewise to a wool comber. Then he came to watch the man scrub the toilets and provoked him further. In the end, the wool comber was flogged bloody for his insolence." Eudes tapped Bertwoin's forearm with a finger. "So if Sir Philippe comes to mock you, remain deaf to his insults."

"I'll stay as silent as a snake," Bertwoin said. "My hope is that the master I serve will oppose him."

Eudes nodded. "Both Sir Jean-Luc and the young *visconte* hold the alchemist in respect. He's as useful to them as a knife is to a cook."

They both hesitated and peered into the gloom as a man near the back wall grunted while moving something heavy.

Not sure how long he would be allowed to remain inside the château's walls, Bertwoin decided not to lose any more time before questioning Eudes. "How did the bellows boy die?"

Eudes crimped his lips in a half-smile at this sudden change in subject. "His name was Didier. He wasn't a bad lad, but he was spirited and full of mischief. Made us all laugh, even the chef most times. He pinch-poached a few almonds, the chef boxed his ear for it, and not long afterward, he fell down in convulsions. Died like a poisoned dog."

"So it *was* poison?" Bertwoin asked.

"No one knows. The chef brought in tasters, but Perter scared them off before they could test all the food and drink."

"What did Arundel do then?"

Eudes shrugged. "I and most of the other workers sampled the food and drink. We discovered someone had been at Master Servay's cider."

"Wouldn't that be a stupid thing for Didier to do?"

"Yes, but the prank fits his nature like a lady's glove. The boy was usually no fool, but he did sometimes think himself as important as a crown prince and could be contrary, despite the consequences."

"Did Arundel strike the boy hard?"

"Nah, it was but a stinging blow. The chef has to keep discipline in his kitchen if we are to serve praiseworthy food at every meal."

Bertwoin smiled. Eudes was loyal to his master, a character trait his father, Clanoud, would value. Unlike Rachel's three other suitors, Eudes wasn't a farmer, so his father didn't quite know how to judge his suitability as a future son-in-law. Normally, his father distrusted anyone who didn't work the land, but Eudes might someday be a chef in a nobleman's or wealthy merchant's kitchen. Even if he never rose above being an experienced cook, he might feed all of his relatives when famine stalked the *visconte's* domain.

"Sounds to me like Didier was spiteful," Bertwoin said. "Such a person often makes enemies."

"Ah, no one ever resented him for long. He could charm a laugh out of a dour saint. But sometimes he thought as a child and acted as a child without considering tomorrow."

"Maybe he believed he could punish the chef and dodge the blame," Bertwoin said, not sure how the boy hoped to do that. "Where was the proof against him? Where was the witness who had seen him drinking from the tankard?"

Eudes chuckled. "That would make his revenge even more delicious. Arundel would know who had done it but could do nothing official about it."

"Still," Bertwoin said, "if caught, he might lose a finger for stealing the cider. At the least, he risked losing his position in the kitchen."

"As to that," Eudes said, "there were whispers that he was leaving anyway. His father wanted him to tend their sheep. If so, his revenge was fox-smart. A quick strike against the chef with no remedy. The cider couldn't be replaced in time to serve it at that day's meal."

"Did Servay forgive having to forgo his precious cider?"

Eudes fluttered his lips as he blew out a scoffing breath.

"Forgive? Does a landlord forgive a rent debt? Master Servay howled like a mad wolf. The chef was called to account and, of course, had to pour the blame on Didier's head. Even now, the seneschal's son wants to punish the dead boy's household because their son drank his precious cider."

"Do you think it was poisoned?"

Eudes nodded. "Probably, but why do it? And how did someone do it? The monks bring the cider from Saint-Papoul themselves."

"The master alchemist thinks Master Servay may have been the real target."

"It makes sense to think Didier drank the poison by mistake. The seneschal's son is as spoiled as a noblewoman's lap dog, but who in the château hates him enough to kill him?" Eudes shook his head. "It's also a grave risk. Everyone knows the master will ferret out the murderer's name."

"If it wasn't the cider, could any of the food Didier pilfered have been poisoned?"

"No, he only stole a few almonds. Those remaining were served and eaten at the feast. No one even had a bellyache."

"Could Didier have been sick?" Bertwoin whispered.

"Maybe, but he showed no sign of it. If he had, the chef wouldn't have allowed him in the kitchen."

"Might he have stolen some other food and eaten something that was spoiled or poisoned?"

"Probably not. The servants brought in tested a goodly amount of the victuals, and we did the rest. No one sickened."

Bertwoin clucked his tongue. "These servants brought in didn't know they were testing the food and drink for poison, did they?"

Eudes's eyebrows lowered. "The chef had to trick them. If the servants had known, they would have thrown the food to the dogs when no one was looking and only pretended to drink the ale and wine." He laughed. "When the pig-sticker told them the truth, they all looked as if they had just swallowed hemlock."

"Did they drink any of the special cider?"

"No, there was none left in the tankard, not even dregs."

Bertwoin grunted in frustration. "So you think Didier drank the cider?"

"I do. When he died he wet himself good. All that piss had to come from somewhere."

"What are you two whispering about?" someone barked.

They turned to see Tolarto slink out of the shadows with the furtive, inquisitive air of a storehouse rat. Bertwoin realized the noise at the back wall had stopped. The scruffy muleteer's tunic now seemed more patches than original cloth, his once white coif was soiled gray, and the stink of ale drifted from the mustache covering his mouth. He looked satisfied with himself.

Eudes quickly said to Bertwoin. "So Rachel is well?"

"Yes," Bertwoin said as if the muleteer were invisible. "We haven't seen your father or mother lately."

Tolarto sneered at Bertwoin and told Eudes, "You would do well to stay clear of her family. You can enjoy her without marrying her."

Bertwoin tensed.

"At least," Eudes hissed, "*her* family is respected and will pay the dowry agreed upon."

Tolarto had cheated his eldest daughter out of her dowry with the result that his son-in-law had sent her back home and refused to treat her as his wife. His two younger daughters, of course, now couldn't find husbands.

The gruff muleteer squared off in front of Eudes, who pulled his knife. Tolarto shrank back, surprised the cook was willing to make this confrontation a death match. Bertwoin stepped up beside Eudes to let the muleteer know he would have to fight both of them. Tolarto didn't pull his knife.

"What were you doing lurking down here in the dark?" Eudes barked in the same tone Arundel would have used.

"If the steward catches you stealing, mule-packer, you'll be missing your left hand," Bertwoin said. Too late, he remembered that Tolarto's brother had lost his hand for poaching. He regretted the cruelty of his words.

The muleteer grabbed the hilt of his dagger. Eudes's knife darted like a snake's head, and its blade pricked the back of Tolarto's hand. The muleteer snapped his hand up to his mouth and sucked the wound.

Bertwoin waited, ready to draw his knife if necessary. He regretted what he had said, but there was no swallowing back his words now.

"Another time, another place," Tolarto muttered and pushed past them.

They followed him up the steps into the sunlight and stood a moment outside the cellar's door. Bertwoin had seen Tolarto enter the kitchen and was surprised because the man and his entire clan, except his wife, carried the reputation of thieves.

Bertwoin bumped Eudes's elbow. "So Tolarto has free run of the kitchen and the cellar?"

Eudes nodded. "He hauls drink and other goods for Tisbe. We use her ale. She also supplies some of our salt and herbs."

"I wonder how much of what he's supposed to haul he keeps aside for himself?"

"Tisbe knows how to count. If anything is missing, she will learn of it." Eudes twitched a shoulder upward. "Besides, what can she do? Few others will hire him, and she doesn't want to see her sister and nephews and nieces starve because he's as worthless as a rotten fish."

"So he enters the kitchen at will?"

"Mainly when he's bringing in salt or herbs. Still, we all watch him to make sure his hand doesn't drift over our tables or shelves and pick anything up." Eudes sighed. "Well, I must be getting back. Remember me to Rachel."

"I will," Bertwoin said and smiled. His sister felt a fondness for Eudes, but like their father, she knew not how to judge him. The idea of becoming a cook's wife scared her. She knew how to run a peasant household because she had been raised on a farm, but Eudes lived in noisy, thriving, closed-in Castellar. Still, marrying him would not part her from all that was familiar to her. She would have her kitchen garden and sheep and poultry.

"By the way," Bertwoin said as he waved at the cellar's closed door. "Is Master Servay's cider stored here?"

"Yes, that's why Tolarto is allowed in here."

"Unattended?"

"We can't watch everyone all the time."

The steward strutted down the narrow passageway, clearly displeased when he saw them together. Did he think Bertwoin might corrupt a well-respected cook?

"You are to work now as a *gongfermor*," the steward told Bertwoin. "You can start with the privies in the Lady's Tower. And be quick about it."

So Sir Philippe had already spoken with the steward, and his punishment was to do the foul work of cleaning latrines. Bertwoin nodded goodbye to Eudes and trudged toward the tower. His brash tongue had outrun his common sense, even after Flowia had warned him to keep his opinions quiet. She would be as peeved as a wet cat.

So tonight when he visited the alchemist and Flowia, he had to tell them that he had angered Sir Philippe and been sent away from the kitchen. His failure would be as unwelcome as the thick stink of shit he brought into their house. Flowia would not walk with him tonight.

✺

BUT BERTWOIN HAD WORKED ONLY LONG ENOUGH TO PUT the stench of a *gongfermor* on his body and in his woolen tunic when the lanky steward, clearly irate, returned. Bertwoin was on his knees on a stone floor of a *garderobe*, cleaning a privy with rags and water.

With the rigid face of one who has been rebuked, the steward said, "The château is short of servers. Go home and return in the morning, wearing a clean tunic that doesn't smell of shit. You are to help serve at tomorrow's feast." He smiled and said as if the thought pleased him, "Let us hope you don't stumble and overturn Sir Philippe's soup."

Bertwoin rose and said nothing. It was clear someone in power, probably Sir Jean-Luc, had learned that the steward had moved him to the latrines and hadn't agreed with the change. He smiled. Sir Philippe would not be pleased at being balked.

"You think this is funny, peasant?" the steward shouted. I'll teach you manners." He lifted the swagger stick decorated with filigreed silver.

Bertwoin stepped forward, blocked the upraised arm, and shoved him backward. The steward sprawled on his butt, his back smacking against the closet's stone wall.

"I'll have you whipped for this."

"Well," Bertwoin muttered, "if that's the way it's to be, maybe I should get my whipping's worth and break your arm for you."

A flash of fear passed through the steward's eyes.

"Tell people of my shoving you, steward, and you'll lose your position."

The steward frowned, not understanding his threat.

Bertwoin explained, "Do you think Sir Jean-Luc will keep someone who can't control a simple plowman? He'd do better to appoint me to take your place. If word of my overpowering you becomes château gossip, you'll be working here," he waved a hand around the small privy, "not me."

"Get out! Out!"

Bertwoin skipped down the tower's slippery stone steps. As he strode across the forecourt toward the eastern gate leading into the streets of the citadel, he saw Eudes leaning against a wall outside the kitchen's door. The cook grinned and waved. Bertwoin waved back, fairly certain he now knew who had found the master somewhere in the château and told him that his plowman spy had been sent off to clean privies.

He must remember to tell his father that Eudes was loyal.

CHAPTER X.

Early the following morning, Perter swaggered into Arundel's kitchen, smug as a well-fed tomcat patrolling its territory. As he watched the chopping and measuring, stirring and mixing, roasting and frying of those in the room, he leaned against the stone doorway, yawned, and gloated at his relaxed leisure while they worked.

Arundel, whose all-seeing eyes kept a constant watch over his domain, frowned at him, obviously annoyed. Then the chef returned his attention to sprinkling chopped rosemary over four fresh, pink salmon fillets, a delicacy that made Perter salivate.

When finished, Arundel covered the fillets with a second skillet and carried them over to a grill cook waiting beside a fire. His task done, he turned and called out, "Bless us and our labor, Saint Perter."

Looking ready to lick his paws and wipe the milk from his whiskers, Perter pushed away from the wall and half-bowed to the wiry chef. Finally Arundel had acknowledged—publicly—that an angel had singled him out with a radiant visit.

Perter raised a lazy right hand and blessed the kitchen with an airy sign of the cross. The rood meant nothing to him.

A stew cook chopping onions ducked her head in thanks. At least this woman understood the singular honor the angel had bestowed upon him.

Perter adjusted the strap of a leather pouch hung from his shoulder and said, smirking, to Arundel, "This kitchen is already blessed, is it not? It has you for its chef. Does it not inherit its fame from your skill?"

The chef frowned at Perter's sarcastic tone and said, "So, did this heaven-sent visit not give you visions? Do you now heal the sick?" He gestured at those around him. "We don't yet see a halo above your head."

Perter wiggled his thick fingers and looked noncommittal to show that circumstances might have secretly changed for him. In truth, he too waited for the reason for this heavenly visit to reveal itself. Why come just to knock him to the ground? What honor was there in that?

Abbot Jehan had questioned Alesta until she was almost falling down with want of sleep. But let the monks and the abbot have their doubts. It was just envy. It irked them that he had been chosen instead of one of them.

"Do you see Didier in heaven?" asked a young bellows boy.

With a knowing smile, Perter said, "Well, it helped that he died a virgin."

A young woman of about sixteen, swan-necked and wearing a red headscarf, started. An older woman also seemed surprised by his words. A knowing look of collusion passed between them.

Everyone knew that virginity related to purity, and purity was the cart that one rode to heaven. Both the Church and Good Folk accept this. So Perter knew these women didn't doubt or quibble against the basic belief but disbelieved in Didier's chastity. Did the young woman know otherwise?

"Or I should say," the butcher corrected himself, "if he had died untainted, it would have aided his afterlife. I fear at the moment there's doubt about the destination of boy's soul." He smiled at the bellows boy. "Your prayers might push his soul in the right direction."

The chef clapped his hands. "Enough. Let God tend to the boy's soul while we tend to the soup."

"And may your soup heal noble souls," Perter intoned.

"So why do you disturb my kitchen?" the chef asked.

"I need to borrow a butcher's knife."

Arundel looked at him from the corners of his eyes. "You always use your own."

"Forgot it. Brought all the others but not my best butcher's knife. You want me to bring you pork or not?"

"Give him what he needs," the chef grumbled to the swan-necked cook in a red headscarf.

Casually, Perter carried the knife and a whetstone she gave him to a table under the great window, its shutters wide open to beam in light. Food already prepared for cooking was set out on the table's top. He saw two defeathered larks stuffed with thyme, beef marrow, shallots, and other spices waiting to be boiled before being roasted. So he had heard right. Today, Arundel was serving Master Servay larks as a peace offering.

Perter smiled and moved aside a leg of lamb so he could set his leather pouch on the table. Then he began sharpening the butcher's knife.

Arundel was now busy sprinkling spices on the salmon fillets. Making sure no one saw him, Perter slipped a stuffed lark out of his pouch and exchanged it for one of those already prepared by the kitchen cooks.

When he finished sharpening the knife, Perter put it and

the whetstone in his pouch. He yawned and pretended to be bored. Then he shouldered the pouch's strap and strolled down the long room, stopping beside the stew cook who had half-bowed to him to watch her scrape rabbit meat into a stew. He inhaled the dish's aroma and smiled at her. She blushed and glanced away, pleased by his attention. She might be useful to him later.

The pig-butcher then strolled out of the hot kitchen, curbing his exultant urge to whistle. Arrogant Arundel was about to get a second shock, one that might damage his reputation. And if all went well, Perter knew how he would blame the murder on another arrogant person.

CHAPTER XI.

Bertwoin reported to the château in a clean tunic and found wiry Arundel ruling the kitchen with a long sieve-spoon which he rapped against heads when he wasn't using it to stir a special soup bubbling in a huge iron cauldron hung over a log fire. Pigs and poultry and long-limbed cranes roasted on spits, thrice-cooked for noble stomachs.

Bertwoin was given a server's leather apron but not told what to do. So he loitered in the kitchen and watched a greasy under-cook pound chicken into a paste before the cook boiled it in milk with rice. He saw two larks roasting on a separate spit, a special dish, and walked over to them. The knots tying their legs together were different. Odd. Was this meant to show they were stuffed differently or did it only mean two different cooks had prepared them?

Perter marched into the kitchen with a pork joint on his shoulder and threw a curse at him. "Still idle as a broken bucket, I see."

"At least it's not my head that's broken."

The head butler, who was readying supplies in the larder, heard them and noticed Bertwoin. So he sent him to the *Cour du Midi* where he was told to put down rushes and strew the floor with violets and clove pinks and rose petals. Ferns already hung on the walls between unlit torches to draw flies away from the food and guests. Bertwoin then set up trestle tables and covered them with clean cloths. Did they always live in such luxury?

The chamberlain assigned him to a waiter with only four fingers on his left hand. How could he carry dishes? Bertwoin and three other servers would work two long tables. They laid out silver spoons, gilded goblets, and trenchers—each with a thick slice of old bread hard as wood on it that would become an edible plate when softened by broth, meat drippings, or ale.

Bertwoin's mouth watered at the sight of the four clay dishes, one for every two guests, as he imagined the meat and poultry and fish he would give to the waiter to set on them. He must take care not to drool into the food.

They also set out silver candleholders in the shape of château towers. Since candles were not needed during daylight, Bertwoin guessed that they were lit to perfume the narrow courtyard. How much did this one feast cost?

Then a man dressed in the *visconte's* red-and-white livery strutted into the sunlit feasting area and blew a brass horn. The head butler and steward began ushering guests to their assigned places. A flower girl at the entranceway gave each woman a pink Michaelmas daisy for her hair.

Bertwoin laughed. He would pick flowers at home before their next meal and give them to his *maman* and sisters.

Sir Philippe came in wearing brighter colors than usual— red hose under a yellow tunic. He was about to be seated when he saw Bertwoin. He told the steward to seat him and another young knight with him at the plowman's table. The steward gave Bertwoin a devilish smile of revenge.

Bertwoin groaned. Now he had to stay as watchful as a hungry owl.

Once the guests were seated, young *Visconte* Raimon-Rogièr and *Viscontesse* Agnes entered with studied dignity and were seated at the high table on a dais at one end. The abbot and Sir Jean-Luc sat on either side of them. Both of the seneschal's children, Mistress Millicent and Master Servay, also sat at the high table along with three other guests.

Pantlers rushed in with bread and jams. On their heels followed butlers with jugs of wine.

Bertwoin was kept busy bringing in the food—meat puddings and blood sausages hot in their grease, venison and eels, salted herrings and pike, roasted cranes, spiced potages, dumplings, carrot and onion jams, as well as sauces fragrant with vinegar and cloves, jugs of mustard, and ginger for sifting over the food. He felt lightheaded with hunger but dared not pinch off a bite or two for himself, though he saw two other servers do so. The tables were piled with enough food and drink to feed his entire village.

Sir Philippe, of course, treated him as a personal servant even though he had his squire and the waiter to serve him. He demanded not only that Bertwoin pour his wine for him but also salt his food. Bertwoin pretended to be clumsy and over-salted the meat, which earned him an elbow jab to the ribs.

People began to laugh and shout as the feast progressed. Knights rivaled one another to see who could eat the most. *Visconte* Raimon-Rogièr considered himself a wit and vied with Itier, the troubadour, in jesting.

As Bertwoin came around a corner of the table carrying a pewter jug of beer to the table, Sir Philippe tried to hook his ankle with his foot. Bertwoin hopped over the extended foot.

"Come on, boy," Sir Philippe shouted at him. "Move those clumsy legs and bring another haunch. I'm so hungry I will eat the odor off of cooked beans."

Bertwoin went to the kitchen and loaded a platter with the lowest cuts of gristly meat he could find. When the companion knight who shared food and salt with Sir Philippe saw what was brought to them, he complained, "You would do well to treat our server better, I think."

Philippe shoved the platter away, his face rigid with anger. "What's this?"

Bertwoin acted confused. "Why, you called for more meat, sir. So I brought it as quickly as I could. Is it not plentiful enough?"

The other young knight said, "Ah, he's new here, Philippe. He knows not how to put aside the choice cuts for our table."

Sir Philippe waved at two other guests Bertwoin had also served. "He's done well enough for them, hasn't he? No, by Lord, he means to insult me by bringing me pig gristle."

Sir Philippe leaped up, nearly upending the bench, though three other people sat on it. Bertwoin stepped back, ready to flee rather than take a beating.

Sir Reginald, who sat closer to the high table, cleared his throat, a sound in the sudden quiet that made most guests glance at him. "What have we here?" he asked. "A meal disturbed?"

"What is the problem?" the *viscontesse* asked.

"This server is surly, Lady Trencavel," Sir Philippe said.

"How so?" asked the *visconte*.

"He brings me inferior meat, Lord Trencavel, and thinks I should thank him for it."

The troubadour said in a fluty voice, "Why must he bring you meat, sir? Do you not carry your own?" Everyone laughed. Even the *viscontesse* smiled.

"So Sir Philippe, are you saying that the *visconte* serves inferior meat?" Sir Reginald asked, and Bertwoin wanted to bow in gratitude to the hostage knight.

"No, you misunderstand me, sir." Sir Philippe smiled at Sir Reginald as if he forgave him for misinterpreting his meaning. "This surly server brings me the scraps that will be given to the peasants and pigs after the feast. He serves it to me in an inferior way."

"Then eat, sir, and quarrel not at my feast," said *Visconte* Raimon-Rogièr. "You endanger our digestion." He smiled. "If he brought food to you in a *superior* way, then his behavior would be worthy of my table, not yours."

Sir Philippe bowed and apologized. "I beg pardon, Lord Trencavel."

There was a collective sigh, and the feast fell back into its rhythm of revelry.

"We're not finished, peasant," Sir Philippe whispered to Bertwoin. "Bring me wine and be quick about it."

This Bertwoin did, making sure he spat in it before he set it on the red-and-white tablecloth near the knight's elbow. Then while harpers played and minstrels sang, Sir Philippe called Bertwoin back constantly. Bertwoin felt like a falcon being trained to return to its master, though the knight used no bait and didn't reward his obedience.

Bertwoin knew Sir Philippe would not forgive the two people who had caused the *visconte* to chastise him in public. Since Sir Reginald was his peer and in some ways, his superior, Sir Philippe's means of punishing him were limited. That meant he would purge most of his frustrated anger on the easier target, him.

Finally, while a traveling troupe danced and sang for the *visconte*; Bertwoin and the others brought out the blancmanges, honey cakes, raisins, and pastries. Master Servay was known to be especially fond of pastries, so besides the two roasted larks, Arundel had also baked a large apple tart for him with a griffin cut into the crust as a decoration. Along with the larks, the dessert was the chef's peace offering. The seneschal's son still blamed Arundel for letting Didier drink his cider at a previous meal.

But before Master Servay tasted his pastry, he vomited his meal and cider on the table in front of him. Dumbfounded, he stared at the partly digested mess with an expression of dismayed wonder.

All the guests sat in shocked silence. Bertwoin felt as if he had been kicked in the stomach. Master Servay put a hand up to shade his eyes, their pupils so enlarged Bertwoin could see them from his table. The seneschal's son kept blinking, and his face was flushed. He fidgeted, unable to relax.

"Cider," he cried, his words slurred as if he were drunk. "I'm parched."

A server hurried forward to pour hard cider into his tankard. Master Servay knocked it over when he reached for it. Brown cider spilled across the striped, linen tablecloth.

At least it wasn't wine. They'll get that stain out even after it sets. Bertwoin chastised himself for having such a silly thought during a crisis. Then he blew out his breath. He must stay alert. Had someone succeeded in poisoning it again?

Sir Jean-Luc gave his son a drink from his own cup. Master Servay had trouble swallowing, though he seemed rabid with thirst. He choked down some of the wine, then rose unsteadily, while a servant pulled back his chair.

The abbot made the sign of the cross. Everyone else sat very still and very silent as if they now attended a funeral feast. Many of the women watched in dismay, each with a hand cupped over her mouth.

In a strained voice, Master Servay yelled, "Since when is the sun blue? This cannot be-"

He fell sideways against his father. Sir Jean-Luc gentled his fall to the rushes strewn across the courtyard's stones. The head butler and Itier rushed forward to help.

"To his room," *Visconte* Raimon-Rogièr yelled.

The troubadour pulled limp Master Servay away from Sir Jean-Luc while the head butler bent low and lifted Master Servay's legs.

Sir Jean-Luc led Itier and the butler, carrying his convulsing son, out of the quiet courtyard. Bertwoin scanned the guests. All of them looked aghast. No one looked pleased or guilty. Who would have done this?

After a moment, the *visconte* signaled for a servant to pull back his heavy chair. He rose and announced, "Forgive my abandoning you before the feast is over, but I am now needed elsewhere." He hurried after Sir Jean-Luc.

Young *Viscontesse* Agnes sat pale and silent, looking at everyone gathered in the courtyard as if she wondered how they had gotten there. It was so still, Bertwoin heard a dog gnawing a bone two tables away.

Hytha rose and walked to her mistress. She firmly took hold of the chair's back and waited. The *viscontesse* threw her maid-in-waiting a look of gratitude and rose. She walked with slow dignity out of the courtyard with Hytha following her.

"Witchcraft," a woman said, and though her voice was little more than a whisper, the word belled across the courtyard.

All of the guests waited. A few sipped their drinks but no one ate or spoke. Bertwoin saw concern on every face.

When high-born Itier came back through the entranceway a few minutes later, his stern expression showed he had put aside his jokes and music.

"The revel is done. Go in grief for the seneschal's boy and *Visconte* Raimon-Rogièr's cousin. Master Servay is dead. May God be merciful with his soul and welcome him into heaven."

Bertwoin watched the guests leave as quietly as moths. He understood why no one spoke above a whisper: they didn't want death to glance in their direction.

He knew what he must do.

CHAPTER XII.

Bertwoin approached Itier, who stood behind the high table with his arms crossed over the chest of his long blue robe. He looked in no mood to talk. Bertwoin hoped his impertinence wouldn't earn him a kick or boxed ear.

He told the troubadour, "If it pleases you, order the servants to leave all of the platters and food and wine as they are. Nothing should be cleared away."

Bertwoin waited with the stench of vomit thick around them until the noble troubadour deigned to notice him.

"Do you think it your place, peasant, to tell your betters what they should do? Are you stupid or has this death addled your wit?"

I would ask the same of you, troubadour, Bertwoin thought. "My wits remain unmuddled. The *visconte* will send the alchemist to solve this murder. And when he comes, the master will want to examine everything exactly as it was at the time of Master Servay's seizure."

"And you speak for the old conjuror?" Itier muttered.

"He does," said a gruff voice.

Bertwoin turned to see the burly *bayle* behind him with his arms also crossed over his chest as if copying, and maybe even mocking, the haughty troubadour's posture.

"So you vouch for him, do you?" Itier asked the lawman as he studied Bertwoin. "Your reasoning trots ahead of us, plowman. Good." A server came into the enclosure at that moment, and the troubadour shouted to him, "Let no one touch the high table, Emile."

Itier smiled at Bertwoin. "I will go tell the *visconte* of this. He will thank me for it. And I shall remember you, plowman." Whistling, the troubadour swaggered away.

"He'll remember himself before he remembers you," the *bayle* said.

"I thank you for standing behind me," Bertwoin said.

"So what now, plowman?"

"Now I run to fetch the master."

The lawman nodded. "Go on then. I'll stand here for a while with Emile and make certain no one disturbs anything. Only the alchemist can find clues in vomit or a tipped-over chair or a drowned fly in a tankard."

Bertwoin hurried down the citadel's grassy slope in a stuttered run. People had already heard of the death and crowded into Castellar's streets where they talked in solemn, worried tones. One or two townsfolk called out to him, wanting news about the château, but he shouted that he was on an errand for the *visconte* and ran past them.

When he came within sight of the alchemist's house and charged through the gap in the mulberry hedge, the geese in the poultry yard took alarm. With their necks stretched high, they spread their wings and squawked hoarsely. The gaggle gathered with their backs to the front wall and blocked his way to the door.

Bertwoin would have shoved a path through them, but Roland stood beside them, defending the yard. He watched

Bertwoin's face with porcine intensity and sniffed the air, the bristles raised along his spine. Bertwoin panted but Roland didn't relax.

Flowia flounced out of the cottage with a knife in one hand, and the geese flowed away from her legs. She smiled when she recognized him, but her expression changed to one of alarm when she saw his face. "What have you done?"

"I need to see the master."

She glanced toward the workshop beyond the hedge.

"I failed," he said. "The seneschal's son is dead. He was poisoned as the master feared he would be."

Flowia shoved through the geese, darted past Bertwoin, and ran to the outbuilding with him following her. She knocked once, then jerked the door open and hopped inside.

The room smothered under charcoal smoke. The master sat, startled, on a three-legged stool in front of the hearth with the sleeves of his linen chemise folded up his forearms to hold back the sleeves of his red robe. He stopped pumping a small bellows that aerated a fire under a brass cup.

Flowia blurted out, "Master Servay is dead. Poisoned."

The alchemist clapped a knobby hand on his white hair. Then he leaped to his feet, knocking the stool over backward, and told Flowia, "Prepare yourself. If this is indeed poison, I have need of you."

Flowia shoved past Bertwoin and ran back to the cottage.

The alchemist lifted the cup off the hearth fire with a pair of tongs and placed it on an area of the dirt floor, which was kept bare of rushes or anything else that might catch fire. He scattered the red-hot charcoal in the hearth.

Turning to Bertwoin, he took off his leather apron and put on his red felt cap. "We must be quick."

Bertwoin told him, "I told Itier he should not allow anything on the high table to be touched. A servant and the *bayle* now stand guard over the table."

"Good lad. You were there then?"

"I was, master. I was serving at the feast when the seneschal's son fell over in a fit."

The alchemist smacked a fist into the palm of his other hand. "I *feared* this might happen, yet I didn't prevent it."

"I'm sorry, master."

"The blame lies with me, not you. Come, you can tell us what happened while we make our way there."

Flowia returned, carrying a basket packed with straw and tinkling glass vials that had wooden stoppers.

The master led them toward Carcassonne, and Bertwoin matched his stride pace for pace, while Flowia trotted to keep up. Bertwoin told them about Servay's vomiting, his thirst, flushed face, his being blinded by the sun, his delirium, and his collapse.

"Who served him?"

"The *visconte's* chamberlain. After the server brings him the food, no one else handles Master Servay's platters or pottery. All plates and bowls are marked with a sign, even those made of metal. *Visconte* Raimon-Rogièr's sign is a lion, and I think Master Servay's is…was a pagan beast. It has the body of a lion with the head and wings of an eagle."

"You have a good eye, Bertwoin. Yes, I know these signs stamped in the silver and pewter. I put them there."

"And you were right in thinking that Didier drank Master Servay's cider," Bertwoin said.

"How so?"

"He was full of drink and pissed on himself when he died."

Flowia chucked her tongue against the roof of her mouth. "It's normal for a body to wet itself when it dies."

"But I think the boy did drink the cider," the master said. "Oh yea, the death I feared has come."

As they crossed the wooden bridge into Castellar, a

soldier marched up to them. "Well met, master alchemist. I am come to fetch you."

"Lead on then," the alchemist told him.

Merchants and tradesmen and clusters of women still thronged Castellar's narrow streets and talked in subdued tones. The soldier pushed a path through the people, who eyed them—the master especially—with respectful attention.

As they began the climb up the slope to the citadel, the alchemist asked Flowia, "Monkshood?"

"I think not, master. Death was much too quick. It might be the work of belladonna, death cherries."

"Ah, yes," the alchemist said. "You use them to ease pain."

"And relieve cramps. They don't grow well in gardens, but every wife knows where she may find them hidden in the woods."

"Many men also, I think," the alchemist said. "Do you know where to find death cherries?" he asked Bertwoin.

"I know to avoid it."

"So you recognize it?"

Bertwoin nodded. He remembered his shock at seeing Master Servay afflicted and feeling helpless. "What is the cure for this poison? Is there anything I could have done to save him?"

"Cause the victim to vomit," Flowia said. "And do it immediately."

"Master Servay heaved like a cat spitting up a hairball. It did him little good."

"After they vomit, crush charcoal in water and feed it to them. But make certain they don't choke. You don't want to drown them. You also can use vinegar or vinegar wine if you have no charcoal. Then give them mustard in water. After that, lay them in a dark place and pray to God for His help."

"Odd that the murderer went after the son and not the father," muttered the alchemist. "The seneschal has many enemies, but his son had few. So did this killer murder the son to punish the father? Or did Master Servay have a deadly enemy? Which one was the target?"

"*Visconte* Raimon-Rogièr also lost a cousin today," Flowia said.

"Well said, daughter," the master praised. "It's possible someone meant to punish the *visconte,* though I think most of us would say that young Raimon-Rogièr is becoming a capable ruler and a shrewd one too. When he can be, he is fair."

"Emeline was a woodcutter's daughter, but Brother Gregorius had no quarrel with her father," Bertwoin said, referring to the previous murder the master had solved. "It was her sins the monk meant to punish, not those of the father."

"True," said the alchemist. "We have no reason yet to doubt that this was a simple murder, and Master Servay was the one the killer meant to punish."

After leading them into the château's forecourt, their soldier escort asked a sergeant for orders.

The sergeant jerked his chin at the Lady's Tower and said, "Take the alchemist directly to Chapel Sainte-Marie. The *visconte* and Sir Jean-Luc and their families are gathered there to pray for Master Servay."

Bertwoin didn't envy the alchemist. It would be a delicate task to persuade the nobles that he needed to examine the body while it was still fresh. They might believe such an examination would desecrate the corpse of their son and brother and cousin.

CHAPTER XIII

"To the kitchen first, then the *Cour du Midi*," Flowia said and started across the forecourt.

Arundel was kneading dough on a side table, his sleeves rolled up and his muscular forearms rippling. He glanced at them, then acted as if they weren't there.

Flowia asked, "Was all the food and drink tested before being served?"

"Who are you to question me?"

"The master alchemist sent us. He is working on behalf of the *visconte* and Sir Jean-Luc. Was the cider tasted?"

"All dishes were tested before they were cooked or bake or roasted. And all drinks were sipped before they were poured."

Flowia nodded. "Still, I must take samples of the victuals you had in the kitchen when Servay was stricken."

"We've already fed everything to the sheep and goats." The chef chuckled. "Our livestock eats as well as our nobles."

"Everything?" Flowia growled. "Even the meat?"

Arundel seemed well pleased that his answer had irritated her. "No, meat was fed to our pigs."

"Did you not know that nothing was to be done until the master alchemist allowed it?"

The chef dismissed her criticism with a flick of his right shoulder. "I heard this was the whim of a plowman." His eyes darted toward Bertwoin, then back to his dough. "I was given no official orders. And I won't let a plowman interfere with my duties. Master Servay's death will bring a swarm of hungry guests to his funeral. They'll expect food, and *Visconte* Raimon-Rogièr must fulfill his obligations as a host. This kitchen will feed them well and not mar his reputation."

Flowia stared at a fireless hearth, breathing hard through her nose, her fingers twittering on her knife handle. "The *viscontesse* will hear of this, cook," she said in a husky whisper. "She may want to know how many more people, high born and low, your kitchen will send into the afterlife and why you hindered the finding of Master Servay's murderer."

Arundel slicked dough off his hands and took a menacing step toward her. Bertwoin stepped between them.

"Out!" Arundel shouted at Bertwoin's chest.

"Not until I have my samples," Flowia said.

A few of the kitchen workers moved toward them.

Bertwoin told the chef, "They won't get to me before I've crippled you."

The workers hesitated.

"Your master will find no poison in my kitchen, wench," the chef said to Flowia.

"No, because you hide the trail and help the killer," Flowia said from behind Bertwoin. "Those who come to the château will soon learn to shun your kitchen, cook. The next to die will be on your head."

"Get out of my kitchen, witch."

Flowia laughed. "A witch am I? Well, your wife had no qualms about visiting this witch when she wanted my help."

Arundel looked stricken, then hatred twisted his face into

a snarl. He jabbed a finger at Bertwoin's chest as if pointing through the plowman's thick body at Flowia. "You'll regret your lies about me."

Flowia sniffed. "Witches know secrets, cook. Remember that. And know that you may not prepare the Christmas feast this year if you hinder us from solving these murders. Nobles will think the food from your kitchen is deadly. Already two people have died, and *you* hide the evidence."

Bertwoin heard her skip out of the kitchen behind him and followed her. In the open forecourt, she shook her fists at the late afternoon sun hanging over the crenellated stone-block walls.

"At the end there," Bertwoin said, "Arundel acted as if you had head-butted him in the stomach. What was that about?"

"I fell into anger," she said and sighed. "I don't like being called a witch or a whore, especially when I tried to help him."

"Him? I thought you treated his wife."

"She came to me, but it was his vigor that needed a remedy, not hers."

"You said 'tried' to help."

"Let's just say, Arundel is still more successful at spending his passion on cooking than his wife."

Bertwoin glanced toward the kitchen and saw Eudes slip outside and hesitate like a fox leaving its den. The cook marched down the knobby stone wall, tapping it with his knuckles like a blind man feeling his way, and disappeared around a far corner.

"Quick, we need to follow Eudes." Bertwoin took firm hold of Flowia's elbow to encourage her not to argue with him.

She frowned up into his face and allowed herself to be propelled across the almost empty courtyard. They found Eudes waiting where Arundel wouldn't see them.

"He's scared," Eudes said in defense of his chef. "If the alchemist finds poison in our kitchen, not even half-starved shepherds will eat porridge cooked by him."

Bertwoin asked, "Could anyone have gotten to Master Servay's cider again?"

"No, it was tasted twice."

"Was any leftover food or drink given to the people?"

"No."

"Arundel said he fed only meat to the pigs," Flowia said. "Was that normal?"

Eudes took a deep breath and let it out slowly. He looked at Bertwoin for sympathy.

"We know you're loyal to the chef," Bertwoin said, "but we must find out who did this. If he's done nothing wrong, it'll benefit Arundel if we find this murderer now. Another death and even the *visconte* will avoid eating anything prepared in your kitchen."

"He's done nothing wrong," Eudes said. "It's just that, well, there was ill-feeling between Master Servay and the chef. The seneschal's son was as picky as a queen's favorite cat. But the chef would never harm the boy. And why would he ever use poison? It points blame right at our kitchen."

Bertwoin hummed agreement. "Was any meat thrown to the dogs?"

Eudes shrugged.

"The meat is of little import," Flowia said. "It wasn't contaminated. Everyone ate the meat. Arundel knows for certain that the meat was safe. Pigs have stomachs like ours. That's why he didn't slop the pigs with anything other than the meat this afternoon."

"Now that I think on it, I might have seen boys haul baskets of food to the Aude. I gave it little attention at the time because of the death."

"If we see fish floating belly-up on the river," Flowia muttered, "we should avoid eating them."

Eudes said, "I must go before I'm missed." He grinned at Bertwoin. "Tell Rachel I think of her often."

"I'll do that. Thank you, Eudes. Your loyalty and honesty commend you."

They waited until Eudes had time to reenter the kitchen, then Flowia led the way across the forecourt and through the keep to the narrow *Cour du Midi*. No one was there except Emile, who still guarded the high table. When she approached it, he blocked her way. "No one is to touch anything here."

Flowia smiled at him. "At least you've done your job well. The master alchemist wants me to take samples of the food and drink from the high table." She tapped her basket, making a few empty vials clink.

"Itier and the *bayle* ordered me not to let *anyone* disturb anything on these tables. They said nothing to *me* about allowing you to take any samples."

Flowia moved aside and looked expectantly at Bertwoin.

He stepped forward to face Emile. "What she says is true. It was for her and the master that the food was not cleared away."

Emile blew out his breath in derision. "So you say, but I need someone with authority to tell me you have permission to disturb the things on this table."

Flowia bit her lip a moment, then said in a calm tone, "Here is what is about to happen, Emile. You will balk me, and Bertwoin will smack you down. Then I will take my samples. And when the master does come, you will be chastised for hindering me."

Emile peered around the empty courtyard like a mouse cornered by a pleased cat.

Flowia pushed past him while he considered his choices.

She set her basket on the table and began taking vials out of it.

"Now, you said the sign of the griffin belonged to Master Servay?" Flowia asked Bertwoin.

"If that is what the pagan beast is called." He waved at the table. "His vomit makes where he sat hard to miss."

"Yes, it seems flies can dine on poisoned vomit without ill effect."

Bertwoin grunted. "My guess is that they thrive on it."

Flowia took a sample of the vomit. "Sheep and goats eat death cherries without even suffering indigestion. I don't believe that is true for pigs. Arundel knows the ways of herbs and medicines as any good cook does. So he too believed that the poisoner used death cherries. He gave his suspicions away when he told us what animals were given what leftovers. But I think he lied. None of the animals were fed anything. He had all of the food thrown into the Aude because he couldn't be truly certain the poison was belladonna."

The alchemist entered the *Cour du Midi* slowly, his long, thin face as solemn as a bishop's at a heretic's trial. "Have you finished?" After Flowia nodded, he asked Emile, "Did Master Servay throw scraps to the dogs?"

"As always, master. There is a mastiff he is…was fond of."

"And this dog did not become sick?"

"No, master, not that I saw, and I have not heard of any dog doing so."

The alchemist scratched his cheek. "So the poison wasn't slipped into Master Servay's stew or meat dishes."

Flowia and Bertwoin glanced at each other. Neither mentioned the fact that they too had already determined this. Emile half bowed to the alchemist as if he had been given permission to leave and darted into the larder.

The master scanned the rows of tables and sighed, "I fear there is little more we can learn here. Now we must ask the chef the names of those who entered his kitchen ere the feast. It is best if I do this."

"Yes," Flowia said. "Arundel has already lied to us. And I was not able to take any samples from the kitchen because he dumped all the food not served or eaten into the Aude."

"He gave none to the poor?"

"Not even stale bread."

"Come, let's go talk with this foolish cook."

The alchemist marched through the larder into the chef's domain like a conquering knight.

Arundel was carefully flaying the skin of a peacock with the feathers intact, so he could replace it after brown-roasting the noble bird. He laughed when the alchemist asked who had entered his kitchen that day.

His tone when he answered begged pity for the sad plight he had to bear. Everyone in the domain that had business with the château thought it their right to enter and disrupt his busy kitchen: farmers bringing game and raw food, their wives, merchants, soldiers, knights, ladies, servants, carters, bakers, butchers, and even the château priest who blessed the food. Nobles came in whenever they felt hunger. He pointed at Bertwoin. "Him too."

"As I feared," the alchemist said. "And do you not often sample the food for flavor before it is taken out and served?"

"Yes, master, I do. We do." Arundel waved around at his living underlings. "The poison came not from this kitchen."

"And the wine?" the alchemist asked. "You sample it too?"

"It was robust and tasted of cherries." Arundel held up a forefinger. "But I only tasted what was served at the beginning of the meal to make certain it hadn't turned to vinegar."

"Yet no one else became sick."

"No one," the chef said with satisfaction. "As always, Master Servay drank his special cider."

The master became alert. "And no one else forsook the wine for cider?"

"Not that I know of. Most prefer wine or ale. Even so, I had a boy sip the cider today just before it was served."

There was a pause. Bertwoin realized Arundel had just admitted that he had tested the cider because he believed Didier had died after drinking from Master Servay's tankard.

"Did he not eat larks?" Bertwoin asked.

"Yes, plowman, we roasted two for him." Arundel said. "I also made a large apple tart he favors. We prepared both of the birds here, and they were never out of the kitchen until they were set in the larder and served."

The master said gravely, "Not his cider then or the larks. What of the apple tart?"

"It too was sampled. And I believe he shared it."

The alchemist shook his head. "Ah well, even if we learn what food was poisoned, that may not point to the murderer. I'm sorry, master chef."

"Sorry, master?"

"People will wonder if your kitchen is safe. And dumping the leftovers into the river before I could see them is the act of a guilty person."

Arundel leaped to his feet and shouted, "We poisoned no one."

The alchemist considered him, his expression grave. "Yet, chef, you did everything you could to make yourself look guilty." He turned and strode out of the kitchen.

As they marched in silence out of the Narbonne Gate and began hiking with choppy steps down the hillside into Castellar, Flowia said, "The chef knows the cider that killed Didier was meant for Master Servay, yet he hid this from us. So the moron hampered us from protecting Sir Jean-Luc's only son." She stopped to look back up the hill at the brooding citadel. "Or maybe not."

"What do you mean, daughter?"

"Hytha once told me Master Servay was the chef's most hated enemy. The boy made it his mission to have Arundel dismissed. He badgered his father to talk with and convince the *visconte* to hire another chef. So is Master Servay's dying not convenient for Arundel? It's possible he didn't poison Didier but repeated the crime to rid himself of an enemy in a high place."

"Even at the risk of losing his kitchen?" Bertwoin asked.

"Arundel was in danger of losing his position anyway if he let the seneschal's son berate him from lauds to compline. Might he not have thought it best to stop Master Servay's insults at all costs? And on second thought, how do we know he didn't poison the cider earlier and suffer bad luck when Didier foiled him?"

CHAPTER XIV.

The following morning, Bertwoin sat on a pine stool in the shade of an elm tree near his father, tying together a fox trap with hemp rope. Skinny-legged Maud ran across their front garden and, smiling up at him with the confidence of a favorite sister, she motioned for him to put his head down so she could whisper something to him. Then she said loud enough for their father to overhear her that Flowia waited behind the barn.

Clanoud spat in the weeds.

Bertwoin, like his father, knew that if Flowia had come to fetch him at their farm, where she was no more welcome than poverty, it was important. He set aside the fox trap and stood up.

"There's work to be done here," Clanoud grumbled.

"The fox won't come before I hear what Flowia has to say."

His father grunted and continued mending the leather on a torn harness. Bertwoin took this as permission to see Flowia, turned, and strode toward the barn.

After five or six plowing seasons, after he had reached his

mid-twenties, he hoped Flowia would become his wife. But would she agree to have him? He was only a simple plowman. She was often more mature than he was, more worldly; she had traveled and was an expert healer. Could he keep her love?

Bertwoin sighed with pleasure when he came around the corner of the barn. Flowia looked pretty as an apple tree, wearing a green, boiled-wool apron over a beige dress with a wimple covering her long braid of black hair. "The master wants a word with you," she said as if delivering a commandment.

"I'd rather it was you who wanted a word," Bertwoin teased.

"I want more than a word, plowman. But right now the master waits for you."

Plowman? Why be so formal? "Can you give me a hint of what he wants with me?" Bertwoin glanced in the direction of the elm tree, though he couldn't see his father with the barn between them. "It'll soften my leaving and add welcome to my return home."

"Someone crept into the château's chapel last night and performed a miracle. He or they stole Master Servay's body while a priest held a holy vigil over it."

Bertwoin made the sign of the cross. "Give me two breaths."

He trotted back to his father and told him why he must leave. He relaxed when his father seemed more pleased than disgruntled, probably because the master alchemist sending for his son brought distinction to their family.

Bertwoin hurried back to Flowia. Without a word, she lifted the hem of her dress off the ground with one hand and glided away like a ghost.

They found the alchemist sitting at a trestle table in his

poultry yard, drinking his morning ale. His smile showed no pleasure.

"Flowia, pour our good plowman a mug of ale." He pointed Bertwoin to a bench across the table from him.

"Thank you, master. Ale is always welcome."

"Yes, welcome like a dear friend." As Flowia set a full mug on the table near Bertwoin's elbow, the alchemist told him, "Someone spirited away Servay's body while a kneeling priest prayed over it, and no one saw the thief take the boy's corpse."

"Not even the priest?"

"Not even he."

"A demon?" Bertwoin asked.

"Ah well." The alchemist accepted the possibility with a sideways twitch of his head. "The *viscontesse* suggested it was more likely an angel. I'm told the bishop has his doubts." The alchemist chuckled, then sighed. "Come, we are summoned to perform magic. Sir Jean-Luc wants to know which it was— a demon or an angel that carried away his son's body. Is the boy's soul in the realm of darkness or of light?"

"What if we can't figure out how the corpse was stolen?"

The alchemist smiled up at the noonday sun. "Why this lack of faith in our abilities, young plowman? Do you not think the three of us are a match for this corpse thief?"

Bertwoin looked him in the eye. "We didn't prevent the murder. And I think no man could have done that."

"Maybe not, but finding out how and by whom the body was spirited away is not the *visconte's* final goal. It is only the first step."

Flowia nodded. "He wants us to name the killer of his cousin."

"It's a problem that will quicken our interest," the alchemist said as he stood up. "Come, we must now be of service to our *visconte* and his grieving seneschal."

CHAPTER XV.

The steward escorted them to the Chapel Sainte-Marie, which occupied the greater part of the second level in the Lady's Tower.

Bertwoin stood inside it with his mouth hanging open. Southern sunlight streamed in through a stained-glass window depicting serene Mary cradling her holy child. He gazed at walls divided into curved sections alternating between pale blue and peony pink. These sections tapered upward and inward to meet in a single point at the ceiling's center.

Bertwoin made the sign of the cross. "This is a worthy place to revere God."

He looked at the trestle bier. It seemed to mock them now that the thief or thieves had cast aside the linen sheet that had covered Master Servay's corpse and left it empty.

Stomping about on the dark-brown floor that reminded Bertwoin of the Aude's fertile mud, the master made certain no plank hid a secret chamber beneath it.

"Was the door locked?" he asked the steward.

"No, but a priest guarded the body all night. He would have known had anyone come into the chapel."

"Did he fall asleep?"

The steward rubbed the back of his neck. "He denies doing so. And even if he had dozed a little during the night, how could anyone move the corpse without waking him?"

"And this was his food tray?" Flowia tapped a studded square of wood on a bench nearest the bier.

"Yes, Sir Jean-Luc said nothing was to be disturbed until after the master had visited the chapel."

"Oh, if only I had been allowed to inspect the body before it was stolen," the alchemist muttered.

"*Viscontesse* Agnes decided that would have desecrated the corpse. Her opinion was seconded by the bishop," the steward said officiously. "Any lady or cleric would object to such sacrilege."

The alchemist growled, "Our murderer accidentally announced his intention of harming the seneschal's son by killing a bellows boy. Yet the second murder occurs because everyone here does their best to prevent me from preventing it."

"The plowman was serving at a table at the time," the steward reminded him.

"Yes," the master muttered, "but he wasn't in the kitchen earlier as I had ordered. He wasn't watching over the food and drink."

"Sir Philippe objected to a plowman having the honor of working in Arundel's kitchen."

"Yet you gave this same plowman the singular honor of serving at the banquet when Master Servay died."

"And he didn't prevent the murder," the steward argued.

Bertwoin asked. "And were you not there too? Yet you not only didn't stop the murder, you also made sure I wasn't in the kitchen so I could guard against it."

The steward smiled. "I will convey your concerns to Sir Philippe when it's convenient."

"Good. And ask him why *he* didn't prevent Master Servay's murder. That is his duty, is it not? To protect those in the château? And ask him why *he* didn't protect Master Servay's body from being stolen."

The steward shook his ornamental baton in Bertwoin's face. "Sir Philippe will hear of this, peasant."

The alchemist patted Bertwoin's arm. "Enough."

Pale with anger, the steward said, "I am needed elsewhere. If need be, I can send someone to attend to you."

"No, no," the alchemist waved him away. "We will only remain here for a short while, then we too must depart. Our task is now to find a murderer who walks through walls."

After the steward had stalked out of the chapel, the alchemist stood a moment near the altar and gazed up at the ceiling's central point. Then he looked at Bertwoin and nodded at the door. Bertwoin strode over to it and jerked it open, but neither the steward nor anyone else had an ear against the door.

"Good," said the master.

Flowia tasted a bit of leftover bread from the priest's tray, then sniffed the tankard. Her eyebrows lifted. She dipped a finger into the dregs and touched it to the tip of her tongue. She then looked at the alchemist and nodded.

"So the priest was drugged?" he asked.

"Yes, I'm amazed someone didn't find the cleric lying unconscious this morning."

The alchemist rubbed his long-fingered hands together. "Maybe someone did but chose not to tell on the priest so as not to bring the wrath of Sir Jean-Luc down on his head. Though I think the cleric will find himself replaced anyway. His failure was great."

"If the priest did come awake by himself this morning,"

Flowia said, "then he was drugged by an expert in the use of belladonna. Someone gave the religieux a delicate dose that only sent him to sleep for a few hours."

The master unlatched a small window and looked out on the forecourt.

"Not this one," he muttered. He rubbed a finger across the stone sill. "The dust here hasn't been disturbed."

The other small window, when opened, showed the sparkling Aude. "Well, well," the master said as he examined the sill. "Swept clean."

He judged the distance between the empty bier and window. "It took a man of strength to do it." He fingered his beard as he again stared up at the arched ceiling. "Of course, it's possible there were two or three thieves."

Standing on tiptoe, he leaned out of the window and scanned the grassy hill that sloped down toward the Aude. "But why steal the body?"

Bertwoin suggested, "It punishes Sir Jean-Luc a second time."

"Yes," Flowia agreed. "Or Master Servay. It denies his soul the solace of lying in consecrated ground. Then again, why must it be either/or? What better way to punish all of the family? Servay's spirit is doomed to wander, and if we don't find his body, none of them can lay him to rest. Rumor of this outrage might even tarnish *Visconte* Raimon-Rogièr's honor."

"And the drugged drink came from the chef's kitchen?" Bertwoin asked.

The alchemist said, "It does seem as though Arundel's kitchen is tied to all of these events. The boy died there, Servay was poisoned from there, and the priest's drugged ale probably originated there."

"You think it was the larks?" Bertwoin asked.

"Yes," the alchemist said. "They were the only food Master Servay ate that was reserved strictly for him. It's possible the poison was added after the filling was tasted and stuffed inside the birds."

"Are we certain no one could have poisoned the hard cider?" Bertwoin asked.

"No, but a brave boy in the kitchen tested the cider before it was served at the fateful meal."

"So Arundel tells us," Flowia added. "Who in his kitchen is dim-witted enough to test food for poison?"

"He may have bribed a beggar boy with food and drink," Bertwoin said. "But how could anyone have poisoned the larks without being seen?" He frowned a moment in thought, then snapped his fingers. "Unless it was the cook who prepared them."

"We *will* need to question whoever that was," the alchemist said. "He or she might also have been in a position to slip something into the priest's ale and thus send the cleric off to Somnus's domain." He smiled at Bertwoin and explained, "The domain of the Roman god of sleep."

Flowia looked unconvinced. "Whoever prepared the larks is the obvious suspect for these murders, yet Arundel hasn't shown any distrust toward anyone in his kitchen."

"He doesn't know that it was the larks that were poisoned," Bertwoin said.

She shook her head. "They were the special food eaten only by Master Servay."

Bertwoin scratched his beard. "What if the seneschal's son ate or drank something before he came to the feast?"

The alchemist hummed. "That's a possibility. One that might mean almost anyone in the château had the opportunity to poison him." He tapped Bertwoin's arm. "Let us go down and walk along the tower's outer wall. I think I know how this body thief performed his miracle.

"And you, daughter, go find Hytha or anyone else you know here. Ask how many people other than the kitchen staff knew Master Servay would dine on larks this day. Also, did he have other enemies besides the chef?"

Bertwoin followed the master down narrow steps slick with age and out through the Aude Gate. They walked around the tower on a path at the top of the steep, grassy slope.

Bertwoin wasn't often alone with the master and thought it an opportunity to learn if the alchemist would ever let go of his virgin. "Flowia seems accepted here."

"You mean, unlike Perter's Éléonore?"

"Oh no, I didn't mean that." Why had the master brought her into the conversation?

"Flowia adores Mary Magdalene," the alchemist said, "because her early life repeated the saint's early life. Her mother was an outcast like the Magdalene. I hope Flowia can alter this cursed pattern that afflicts the generations of her family. It is one reason I bought her out of slavery."

"It was kind of you to do so, master."

"I could not do otherwise and expect a place in heaven. She has done well to be so respected as a healer and for her knowledge of plants."

"If she marries, might that not help her escape this curse?"

"I shall consider that. Marriage has its own pitfalls."

Just off the path under the second chapel window the master had opened, something had crushed the broom and flattened the dusty weeds.

"So," the alchemist said, "the thief or thieves shoved the corpse out of the small window. Much easier and safer than lugging a burdensome body down slippery steps."

The alchemist waved at a little-used dirt road circling the bottom of the slope. "He or they probably had a cart ready to carry away the body." He smiled at Bertwoin. "Something not demon or angel would need."

116

He glanced up at the sunlit sky. "We haven't had rain for a few days, so the possibility of footprints is scant, but let us search the slope anyway."

They found drag marks but little else. Still, the master said he felt confident he could now prove that a strong man or men, not a demon or angel, had stolen Master Servay's corpse.

CHAPTER XVI.

While butchering a lean, scalded boar in the sunny forecourt, Perter watched the steward meet the nosy sorcerer, the smart-mouthed plowman, and the virgin witch. He then watched the four of them march with grim purpose to the Lady's Tower.

That probably meant the alchemist didn't believe the silly rumor that an angel had winged the seneschal's whelp to heaven. Good. He hadn't poisoned the scamp to have him celebrated as a local saint.

Perter touched his head where the angel had blessed him. At least, it didn't hurt anymore. Maybe he should pretend to be blessed with visions. Ugly Thea made a good living swindling religious idiots. Why shouldn't he do the same? He needed to talk with Alesta and Éléonore about it. They'd have ideas.

Right now, his goal was to keep one step beyond the alchemist's claws. His stealing the body from under the nose of a doddering priest had baffled the *bayle*. The old ex-crusader was smart enough for common crimes but couldn't go bone-deep enough to solve a theft or killing carried out by someone who had imagination.

But the sorcerer hunted with keener wit. He had caught at least three murderers before now, and one of them had been as clever as King Solomon. But then, what if the old conjuror did divine how he had spirited away the brat's corpse? That didn't mean he knew *who* had carted the body away. He must make sure that this time the alchemist's magic failed.

Still, it was wise to be cautious. Tonight, he'd haul the body out of its barrel and get rid of it. Perter glanced at a bucket of pig organs and grunted a chuckle. Another surprise awaited Sir Jean-Luc and the hoity-toity château nobles who used people then threw them aside as if they were privy rags. The sweetmeat of revenge just kept getting tastier and tastier.

Perter set aside cuts of meat instead of carrying them to the kitchen. If lordly Arundel wanted his pig parts immediately, he could damn well send a boy out to fetch them. Right now, it was important to remain in place so he could watch how the alchemist dressed out the situation.

The steward pranced out of the Lady's Tower soon enough, and not long afterward, the trio of thief-catchers also showed. The witch sashayed toward the main hall while the sorcerer and his pet ox scuttled toward the Aude Gate and its barbican. So the old fox had figured out how he had whisked the body away. That was quicker than a blink. Had the old heathen used Devil's magic? Probably not. Even a pagan like him wouldn't risk such brazen sacrilege in a chapel. Of course, it was all religious nonsense anyway. The Church served the Evil God.

Perter hurried to finish butchering the hog but was only three-quarters done when the alchemist and plowman marched back into the courtyard. The alchemist strode toward the keep, probably to report to Sir Jean-Luc. The swaggering plowman loitered near the main building until the witch swished outside again. They strolled across the fore-court, close together, ignoring everyone, she laughing at what he said, and he intent on entertaining her. So that was how it was between them. Perter grunted. Here was a scrap of gossip for Alesta and Éléonore. Was the alchemist's virgin still a virgin?

It was the quiet time of the afternoon when Perter finished cutting up the boar and delivered the last of the meat to the almost empty kitchen. As he was washing his knives, the alchemist shuffled out of the keep.

Perter followed him out of the château, almost treading on the heels of the alchemist's sandals. He needed to get home. He had more butchering to do this day.

THAT NIGHT UNDER A HALF MOON, PERTER CARTED THE barrel with Servay's body lumped inside it to a crumbling Roman wall of weathered ash-gray stones. It lay in the woods at the edge of Clanoud's land. He rolled the barrel across rough ground to a maple tree with sturdy limbs.

There he opened one end of the barrel, gave it a moment to exhale the stench of death, then pulled out the naked corpse with its mushroom-like skin. A few curious pigs came grunting out of the woods. Perter tied a hemp rope to the body's ankles, threw the loose end over a sturdy limb, and hauled the body upside down into the air.

First, he hacked off Servay's left arm. He had never cut up a *human* body before, and though it might be more inter-esting than just butchering one more hog, he doubted it would be as difficult. With this corpse, he didn't have to worry about different cuts of meat.

He sliced the flesh off the arm and tossed it to the squealers to give them a taste for the meat. Their celebratory noise was like blowing the dinner horn; hogs swarmed out of the restless bushes. He glanced in the direction of the house, which was out of sight. Clanoud probably couldn't hear his swine and would dismiss the noise if they did.

Perter sliced open Servay's soft belly, enjoying his unusual labor. Most of the organs resembled those he found in pigs. After he ground them up for sausages, he would have no trouble substituting them for minced hog meat. Would it taste the same? Pork was succulent meat. He stuffed the organs into a hemp sack and hung it from a limb out of the porkers' reach. Laughing, he slapped the squishy bundle. Oh yes, he had a special plan for Master Servay's innards.

Using his meat ax, Perter hacked the other arm into pieces and tossed them to the enthusiastic swine. It lifted his heart to watch them fight over the boy's arm. Did the flavor of Saint-Papoul cider sweeten this taboo flesh?

The grunters didn't care how he carved up the corpse or which cuts he served them, so he rough-cut the torso into sections and let them fight over the parts. He castrated what little remained and stuffed the shriveled testicles, which he judged as rather small, into the hemp sack with the organs. They would add spice to his surprise for the seneschal. Then he chopped up the legs. The pigs did the rest; they were adept at stripping a corpse to its bare bones.

He kept Master Servay's head. Alesta would think of something wrathful to do with it. She was clever that way. And joyful Éléonore would dance and sing as she gloried in her wicked and delightful revenge.

Perter began carting the empty barrel, the head, and bloody sack of forbidden meats away. His horse had been nervous around the feeding swine and was eager to return home. Tomorrow on the way to the château, he might walk this way to see if the pigs had licked the bowl clean.

Now was the time for his women to mince and spice and cook what little remained of Sir Jean-Luc's spoiled brat. Even without a body, the *visconte* was sure to offer a funeral feast for his cousin, the seneschal's son. Perter chuckled. With luck, Arundel would cook and serve the nobles more in his sausage than anyone knew.

Somehow those in the château must learn later that they had taken part in a blasphemous rite of cannibalism. As the Church's priests said, "This is my body, which is for you: this do in remembrance of me."

Let them eat their child as a sow eats her dead piglet.

CHAPTER XVII.

S oft-footed as a stray cat, Bertwoin served at the solemn feast that followed a requiem mass for absent Master Servay. Nobles from everywhere in the *visconte's* fertile domain—from crowded river towns to isolated forest fortresses—swarmed into the château's forecourt, now set up with trestle tables, the normal red-and-white table-cloths replaced by black ones. The *Cour du Midi* had proven not large enough to hold the multitude.

A priest read Bible verses while the guests ate, and conversations were muted to a beehive murmur. Many guests may have wondered if one requiem mass was enough to tuck Master Servay's wandering soul into its eternal rest. His body lay unburied in sacred ground. If it was found, would a second remembrance ceremony be required? The Good Folk clustered among the mourners may have wondered what newly pregnant woman now hosted his soul. Of course, it might have flitted into the womb of a nearby mare or ewe or some other she-beast.

Sir Jean-Luc slumped at the high table, staring straight ahead as if contemplating the divine judgment laid against him: his being condemned to lack a male heir. He politely ate a few morsels of the ritual meal the chamberlain set before him, but it was the dogs, animals, and poor people who would thrive on his food today. His appetite lay like a stone in his stomach. His daughter, Mistress Millicent, copied her father's reticence and sat rigid-faced as she stoically endured this public, familial duty.

From a table near the kitchen, Sir Philippe watched Bertwoin with spider-like concentration. Bertwoin, fortunately, had been assigned to another table and made sure he always approached the kitchen without passing near the glowering knight.

But today's reprieve only delayed Bertwoin's impending punishment; it didn't repeal it. Sir Philippe didn't need to attack him during this pensive banquet, not after the steward had told Bertwoin that his service was needed longer. He would continue working at the château until after the Christmas feast. Flowia had told him that a willing back was often used, but it was the back of Bertwoin's neck that itched now and warned him that something was amiss.

When he spoke to Bertwoin, the steward had kept his expression bland as milk and his manner officious, though his eyes glowed with curdled spite. Bertwoin assumed this need for his further service originated with Sir Philippe, and its intent was malicious. It confined him for hours each day inside the château's impregnable walls, a place where the spiteful knight held sway, a place where the low-born rabbit huddled in a cage prowled by a noble wolf.

Near the end of the meal, Bertwoin paused in the kitchen's doorway and looked at the people who had gathered in the forecourt for leftovers from the feast. Perter stood a little apart from the crowd, a foxy smile of amusement on his face as if he knew a secret. Had he too come for scraps? No, the château servants knew not to give food to his household.

The pig-man locked eyes with him and didn't look away until Bertwoin did.

WHEN BERTWOIN CAME HOME LATE THAT AFTERNOON, HE found his father lounging like an emperor on a rotting cherry tree stump beyond the kitchen garden. His *maman* was picking lice out of her husband's thinning hair and crushing them between her thumbnails. Bertwoin decided to delay asking for his father's advice about being at risk in the château. He didn't need to make his *maman* fret.

He had agreed to give her what coins he earned, having little need for them himself. This soothed his father's ruffled discontent with his doing less work around their farm. His brother, Wilfraed, and Uncle Laurence found themselves doing most of his daily chores now that, as they complained, an ox had become one of the *visconte's* greyhounds.

Would he shame his family? He doubted he would attend and serve at the joyful Christmas feast. After Sir Philippe punished him, he was more likely to be banished from the château or find himself shivering inside a dungeon cell instead of bringing food into the *Cour du Midi*.

His father grunted on seeing him. "You need to fetch a stout ax handle. We've work to do tonight. And be certain you bring your knife."

"Work at night?"

"Don't piss yourself about it. Just be ready after dark to do what I tell you to do." He smiled. "It won't harm your grand position with the *visconte*."

So not long after sunset, Bertwoin wrapped himself in his woolen cloak, fetched an ash ax handle from their barn, and followed his father, who carried a walking stick also made of ash. It was a bone-breaker and long enough to give him a decided advantage over a man wielding a mere cudgel or even a dagger.

The night purred, and the breeze felt as soft as a woman's lingering caress across Bertwoin's cheek. The half-moon's light made it easy for them to avoid fallen limbs. His father strode along a forest path quiet as a fox so as not to catch the notice of demons or imps. They were known to prowl this part of the woods after sunset.

They circled Montredon and took the road out of their village toward the *visconte's* mill. There they joined a group of three silent monks, four restless townsmen, and a few ruffians who stank of sweet ale. Mist ghosted off the Aude, drifted past them, and crept into the silent forest.

The *bayle* marched up to them and studied the group, judging the men. He nodded to Clanoud, his fellow ex-crusader.

"Listen well," he said. "The Good Folk are gathering tonight on Drouet's place. They mean to hold a worship service in the clearing where the Widow's Altar stands."

Bertwoin glanced at his father. Why were they here? They had no quarrel with the Good Folk. They didn't share their beliefs, but that wasn't reason enough to harm any of them. It was God's right to punish or forgive the Good Folk's heresy, not theirs. So why had his father agreed to come tonight? He respected many of them. They worked as weavers and led simple lives. They followed the way of the Apostles, unlike the Churchmen who wore silk and lived in palaces and taxed the poor.

The *bayle* put his hand on the hilt of his sword. "Stay on the deer trail behind me. They'll probably keep to the main paths when they come. Move like the thieves I know some of you are. I don't even want to hear a fart."

The ruffians laughed, the townsmen looked uneasy, and the monks looked aghast.

"They should all have gathered by the time we get there," the lawman said, "but we don't want a latecomer bumping into any of us and raising the alarm."

"They'll remember if they bump into me." A barefooted ruffian slapped his club into his empty hand. Smiling, one of his companions bumped his shoulder.

The *bayle* held up his hands to silence them. "When we get there, we'll surround them."

A clownish ruffian twisted his butt to one side and farted, making everyone laugh except the three monks who looked ready to hiss at such levity.

The *bayle* said, "Do nothing, *nothing*, until I shout the order for you to charge in." He patted his sword. "Remember what you hear and see. The bishop and abbot will want your evidence at the trial."

So they had come to serve the Church, not the *visconte*.

A young monk, his mouth a little lopsided as if it had been slapped out of kilter, turned to face the men awash with moonlight. "They believe not in the saints and do unnatural acts and eat the ashes of babies in their rituals. They-"

The frowning *bayle* cleared his throat to stop the interruption. "When I yell the order, rush in. Grab their priests. We'll also need one or two of the followers."

"They preach heresy," the young monk brayed with righteous zeal. "Their souls are lost, damned. They kiss the asses of cats."

"What?" Bertwoin argued. "They follow the ways of the Apostles. No Apostle did that."

His outburst shocked the monk to silence, and they all listened to the watery murmur of the Aude. Clanoud slapped his knuckles against Bertwoin's chest. For half a breath, the *bayle* looked amused.

The sermonizing brother pointed a trembling finger at Bertwoin's face. "Blasphemer! You're one of them."

Clanoud rounded on him. "He's as firm a believer as you are, yapping monk."

The brother flinched back a step, and a laughing ruffian whooped, "Watch yourself, black-robe. Their family punches monks on the nose."

"We're here to disband a Good Folk's meeting, not fight amongst ourselves," the *bayle* said. "So calm down. And remember to capture their relics."

The young monk lifted his face cloudward. "It will not be a sin to touch their false idols," he blatted. "These objects cannot defile you with their evil. God will protect you."

"Yes," drawled the *bayle*.

"Tonight," the monk continued, "you do the work of the true Church. Tonight, you will please God. Tonight, you will lead the heretics back onto the path of righteousness or tumble them down the slippery slope into Hell."

An older monk patted the young brother on the shoulder and told the group, "Many of these people are just neighbors who have strayed. Once caught, most of them will repent. Now let us pray for God to look favorably upon our endeavor."

After the prayer, the *bayle* again cleared his throat. "As the brother here said, they're our neighbors. We're not going to this meeting to crack heads or break bones. We mainly want to capture their leaders. You will know them by their black robes and the look of starvation on them."

A ruffian looked at the eager young brother and said, "I hope none of us mistake our black-robes for theirs."

"More reason," the *bayle* muttered, "for us not to bash any heads. Only use your weapons for self-defense."

Again Bertwoin wondered why his father had agreed to come. The Good Folk caused them no harm. Both Flowia and the alchemist tolerated them, as did *Visconte* Raimon-Rogièr. It was not uncommon on the streets of Bourg or

Castellar or St. Vincent to see believers, *credentes*, greet one of their priests by dropping to their knees and bowing three times. Many noble families had Good Folk among their members, especially among the women. His father's sister was a *credente*. So why were they here?

The *bayle* led the men along the Aude's grassy bank toward Montredon, retracing the route Bertwoin and his father had taken. Drouet was their neighbor. The men stalked through the quiet night, each following the man in front of him.

When they entered the quiet woods of Drouet's farm, Bertwoin heard a murmur. As they neared the clearing, he realized the sound was the raised voice of a woman. Then he recognized Gertrude's voice. His stomach fluttered as if a moth were trapped inside it. They had come to capture her, a Good Folk priestess. She was the mother of Roqua and mentor to Emeline, the two young women who were murdered last season.

Who had betrayed her tonight? Tolarto? Probably not. He had betrayed the Good Folk before, so they, and especially Gertrude, knew not to trust him.

As Bertwoin slinked down the path toward the Widow's Altar, he saw the faint light of the Good Folks' fire. The *bayle* stopped at the front of their line and whispered something to the old monk behind him. The men passed the order to spread out and surround the clearing down their line, then dispersed into the woods where prickly bushes snatched at their woolen cloaks. Limbs scratched across the palms they raised to protect their faces.

Bertwoin sneaked along behind his father, following more by sound than sight. He was appalled at the noise he and the other men made. It seemed only the deaf could fail to hear them. But Gertrude preached in the clearing with loud fervor.

Peasants, villagers, and artisans sat in circles around her black-robed figure. She preached with the husky authority of a prophetess and gestured with skeletal hands that flashed white as bone in the wan firelight. Bertwoin thought of Mary Magdalene, the woman in the Bible Flowia adored most. The Good Folk said Mary had also preached in this way. Many of them also believed she had been more than just a disciple to Jesus: she had been his wife.

The Good Folk had set up an ornate Tree of Life on the flat boulder called the Widow's Altar, which was now draped with a white cloth. A valuable codex, probably a Good Folk Bible, lay centered on the altar. The three abbey monks who had come with them would want to seize both the tree and the book and use them as evidence before they burned the heretical objects.

Bertwoin crouched behind a bush, its leaves trembling in the timid breeze, and scanned the fifty or so people in the clearing. When the *bayle* ordered them to charge forward, he would do so but not catch anyone.

Bertwoin stopped breathing. Nearly all of the Good Folk wore cloaks with their hoods raised to protect them from the night's damp chill. He wasn't certain but the dark green wool of one cloak with a peaked hood looked familiar. If so, why had she come?

Gertrude stood tall behind the altar and incited the *credentes* to follow the ways of righteousness, her melodious voice both confident and joyous. "And I tell you that the soul of a newborn babe is ancient."

Bertwoin had expected the sect members to be dancing themselves into trances around a fire and ranting in revelatory tongues. Instead, they listened as docilely as grazing sheep. And they could understand every word of her sermon because she spoke Occitan instead of the Church's Latin.

Bertwoin plunged through the woods to position himself

behind the woman in the green cloak. If it was Flowia, he must be in place before the *bayle* ordered them to charge in among the worshippers. He, not some ruffian, had to capture her. Then in the confusion, he would slip her into the dense woods and escort her home.

"Did not Jesus Himself say that John the Baptist was Elijah come again?" Gertrude shouted. "These truths are kept hidden from you by Rome's corrupt priests. And why waste your breath confessing to these charlatans? Only the Good God can forgive your sins. No mortal man can do this for you. No, these priests serve the vile god who created this Earth. They lust after-"

"Blasphemer!" shrilled the young monk. Waving his dagger about like a madman, he rushed into the fire-lit clearing.

Bertwoin stood stunned. Good Folk women leaped up screaming; their men rose, yelling curses. The edges of the Good Folk crowd melted away into the dark woods. Gertrude raised her arms heavenward. The cowl on her robe dropped behind her neck when she stared up at the low clouds, her white face radiant as she gave herself up to a martyr's fate.

Bertwoin rushed into the clearing as did the others with him. He ran after the woman in a green cloak, who dodged around a townsman from their group and faded into the sheltering forest. The townsman trotted after her, but Bertwoin outraced him and plunged into the woods after her.

Bertwoin chased her through the undergrowth, throwing himself into the light patches between dark shrubs, following her as he had his father, more by sound than sight. Her crackling flight through the bushes grew louder as he closed the gap between them. A tree limb whipped around his raised hand and slapped his cheek and he cursed.

Her sound stopped. People still shouted behind them in the clearing, but she made no noise. Was she hiding? A smart thing to do. He too stopped; he must not corner her before she recognized him. Flowia might use her knife.

He whispered her name.

"Bertwoin?"

"So it *is* you," he said as he crept with more confidence toward where she hid.

"And it's *you*. Why are you pursuing me?"

"It's better that I catch you instead of some of the men I'm with," he said, still moving toward the sound of her voice.

"And why would you be here with them?" she snapped.

She was acting like he was the one at fault. "I don't know," he said. "My father forced me to come."

He found her behind a sturdy tree trunk and touched her shoulder but she angrily knocked his hand aside.

"Why does your father hate the Good Folk?"

"He doesn't. I don't know why we came or why the *visconte* sent his *bayle* on this raid. But why are you here? You're a Christian. If you're caught, the master will be furious with you."

"They're Christians too. And I go where I will." After a pause, she poked his stomach with a forefinger. "I came to listen, to hear what it might have been like to hear Mary Magdalene preach," she said, her tone less angry now.

> "I came to heed what Gertrude had to say
> and I don't agree with all her beliefs, forsooth
> but a measure of what she did convey
> belled with the resounding ring of truth."

Bertwoin relaxed. Her rhyming meant she was less angry now. He decided not to point out that if she were caught it would embarrass the master. He glanced back toward the clearing where faint firelight showed. The noise there was now a joyless murmur.

"Should I walk you home?"

She hesitated, then said, "No, you'll be missed."

He sighed. "Ah, you're right, and my father isn't one to accept excuses."

He moved against her, and when she didn't pull away, he found her cheek with his searching fingers and kissed her, then hugged her. "I'll still walk you home," he said, his voice husky with longing. "A beating is a trifling price to pay."

"It's best if you're not missed," she whispered and slipped out of his embrace.

"Do you not fear what might lurk in the night woods?"

"You mean men with clubs and knives?"

"No, I mean things more dangerous than us."

She twittered a mocking laugh. "An angel watches over me."

"Well, fly away with your angel then."

She glided away from him, then stopped hidden a few paces away in the dark and said, "Fly? That reminds me of what I learned about the larks."

"Larks? We should be more interested in larking than in discussing larks."

She shushed him. "Nearly everyone in the château knew Arundel was preparing the larks for Master Servay as a peace offering."

"So?"

"So the poisoner doesn't necessarily have to be numbered among the kitchen staff. Good night, dear plowman."

He listened to her swish away through the shrubbery.

When he returned to the clearing, he discovered the raiding party had captured only three sect members: two doddering women and emaciated Gertrude. His father saw him return alone and eyed him with silent suspicion. But it didn't look as if his father had taken any prisoners either.

Like him, none of the others, not even the ruffians, had

been eager to capture their neighbors and turn them over to the Church. And he must remember that the *bayle* had never shouted the order for them to charge into the Good Folk gathering. Bertwoin assumed the monks had caught the three prisoners, all of them women.

The two elderly women stood with their heads bowed, their faces hidden. Gertrude kept her hands tucked into her sleeves like a humble monk and stared straight ahead. Her face, pale as a grub's body, was serenely resolute.

Her last daughter, little Marthe, had died two Sundays ago. Her entire family, except Roqua who was killed by a God-crazed monk, had died of the spitting-blood disease. So now Gertrude lived alone, the last fading blossom on her family tree. No relative dared move in with her because they feared the deadly sickness would infect them.

Normally, the *visconte* would have given her house to a family with men who could work his fields and soldier for him if need be. But several Good Folk men and women volunteered to do the labor required of Gertrude. *Visconte* Raimon-Rogièr found he could work several men instead of just the three or four men normal in a single household.

The bishop, of course, resented the fact that the *visconte* allowed this female heretic to live and preach in the domain. Her capture would please him. Now the Church could rid his holy diocese of her.

"What have you done with Master Servay's body, devil worshipper?" the gloating young brother asked.

"What?" Gertrude fluttered her hands. "Us?"

The other two women prisoners stared wide-eyed with horror at the monk.

"We know you need sacrifices for your rites," the brother said. "Who but an evil sorceress could spirit away his body?"

Bertwoin swallowed. Did the Church mean to blame Master Servay's murder on the Good Folk?

Gertrude pointed an accusatory finger at the monk's face. "It was one of you who killed my Roqua, and to hide its guilt, the Church blamed her murder on another. Now, you wish to blame us. Does that mean the Church is guilty again? Did one of your accursed flock kill the seneschal's son?"

"It's your abominable sect that is cursed," the young brother sneered. "God will punish you for your crimes, heretic."

"Not as much as He will you, monk," she said in a tone laced with gentle pity.

"You, a woman, cannot know the ways of the true God."

She nodded. "But I know the truth taught by the early Church before your popes profaned God's words so they could gain power." Her expression hardened into contempt. "A puffed-up little ant like you knows not what God does or thinks."

Some of the men grinned.

"And a day will come when you grovel, monk," she said. "Even a tapeworm in a black robe bleeds when cut."

The monk made the sign of the cross to protect himself from her profane words.

CHAPTER XVIII

After the aborted raid on the Good Folk, the *bayle* ordered the monks to take the female prisoners to the dungeon in Bishop Othon's palace. They looked pleased to do so.

As he watched them herd the three cloaked women away, the *bayle* muttered to Clanoud, "They want praise from the bishop for bringing in heretics. Let them have it. The *visconte* wants no part in this, and neither do I." He rubbed his hands together as if washing them, then pretended to flick drops off of his thick fingers. "Neither do I," he repeated.

Clanoud said, his voice droning with sarcasm, "It was a shame, a real shame when that fanatic yelled and charged into the gathering. He ruined our chance of catching more prisoners."

The *bayle* clicked his tongue as if disappointed. "Yeah, he'll carry the blame for it. When Bishop Othon points a furious finger at our young *visconte's* nose and accuses him of neglecting his duty, of not purging heretics from his domain, he'll learn that a young monk spoiled our outing. The good bishop will then blaze up like a dry bonfire.

"Word will come down to the abbot telling him our scrappy young monk needs to learn discipline. The boy's knees will be nothing but bleeding sores from kneeling on stone floors as he begs God's, and the abbot's, forgiveness. And God might be a little more forgiving. The monk will gag on the stink of shit while he cleans the abbey's latrines."

The lawman smiled at Bertwoin. "It's a common punishment for those who anger their betters."

How many other people know I cleaned privies at the chateau?

Raising his voice, the *bayle* told everyone, "Come, let's wake Tisbe if she be abed and drink ale to her profit. The bishop pays tonight."

The ruffians, whose only payment would be in drink, cheered and swaggered away in laughing camaraderie. As Bertwoin followed them, he wondered if the wily *bayle* had asked his father to come on this raid because he knew Clanoud would have no intention of catching anyone. Bertwoin's *credente* aunt was a widow with four sons and three daughters. She may have attended Gertrude's gathering tonight.

Had the *bayle* purposely picked men who wouldn't be eager to catch Good Folk heretics? Of course, he had to accept the monks that the abbot had sent.

Tisbe had four trestle tables outside her front door where her croft would have been and sold ale or wine to those who came to sit at them. Many men also visited Tisbe's two bedrooms where a couple of young prostitutes sold their bodies for others' pleasure.

The self-satisfied *bayle* sat down at a trestle table with Clanoud, Bertwoin, and three of the townsmen—a shoemaker, a carpenter, and a dyer. The ruffians and the other townsman kept their own company at two other tables.

Tisbe opened a shutter and peered out at them, then strolled outside, smiling, with a people's lawyer trailing behind her. He nodded to his cousin, the *bayle*, then strutted away pompous as a rooster.

Tisbe lit candle lamps for them, then without being asked, hurried back inside and brought the *bayle* ale in a leather tankard reserved only for him. He took breakfast every morning at her tavern, so it was here that people came to see him with complaints or to report crimes.

"The bishop is the host for our amusement tonight," he told her.

She hesitated. "You'll see he pays?"

"I'll see to it."

Tisbe smiled at Bertwoin. "You can help me serve, Ox." She winked at him and said, her voice lowered into a seductive tone, "I'll remember you for it."

The men oohed at his luck. His father, laughing, elbowed his arm. "Just pretend we're nobles at the château."

Despite himself, Bertwoin blushed as he stood up. He kept out of Tisbe's reach when he ducked into her front room to fetch clay bowls and pitchers of ale, but Tisbe was all business now and barely looked at him. When done helping her, he sat down beside his father and poured himself a bowl of red ale.

"Well, we beat the hay," the dyer sitting at their table said, "and the rats ran out in all directions. Yet all we caught were three half-lame women." He shook his head in mock despair. "Ain't that a pisser?"

The shoemaker tapped on the table. "It was Church business. We'll be blessed for it. And I recognized some of those Good Folk. Perter and his wife and Gertrude's sister, Éléonore, were right up front but got away."

The *bayle* flapped a dismissive hand to show the cobbler's evidence wasn't welcome. "They'll deny being there. Then it's just their word against yours."

"But the Good Folk don't lie," the shoemaker joked in a syrupy voice. "They confess instead."

Clanoud harrumphed. "I don't think Perter has accepted that part of their holy script yet."

"No, indeed," said the *bayle* with satisfaction.

"We should've waited until they drank their potions," said the shoemaker. "Then after they fell down in trances, we could've loaded them up for the bishop like barrels on a cart."

The dyer wiped ale from his mouth. "I'd like to catch Éléonore in a trance while she's out in the woods."

"She was once married to a mighty man," said the *bayle* in an offhanded way. "Men like Egbeurt come around only once or twice in your lifetime. Staunch in battle and steady in camp." The *bayle* stared off into the cloudy night for a breath or two. "True, Clanoud? You fought Egbeurt once, I recollect. He didn't best you by much."

"It was enough."

"It was a sight to see," the *bayle* said to Bertwoin, yet loud enough for even the ruffians to hear. "Your pa and Egbeurt. Two lions fighting over what? Who knows? Probably Éléonore. But I remember the brawl, all right."

He looked at the middle-aged carpenter, who smiled and nodded to acknowledge that he too remembered it. The *bayle* clasped his hands over his belly and sat up straight, well content to have an audience for his memories.

"Egbeurt was sitting across the table from Clanoud here when he stood up and clouted him. Knocked Clanoud backward off his bench. Then Egbeurt sat back down. One blow from him was usually all it took. Usually. But not with this one." The *bayle* jutted his bearded chin toward Clanoud.

"Our man here got up and flung himself over the table at Egbeurt, who was one surprised cat, I can tell you. They wrestled and pummeled each other and shouted curses that probably shocked the ladies embroidering in Château Comtal clear on the other side of the Aude."

The *bayle* paused to sip his ale before he again looked at Bertwoin, his eyes twinkling in the candlelight. "Your pa and Egbeurt fought and clawed at each other like bears, wild-eyed and half insane with rage. In the end, it was Clanoud who couldn't get up, though he tried."

After an appreciative moment of silence, the *bayle* nodded wistfully. "I was younger then. Still had my full strength. With the help of a few others, we kept Egbeurt from stomping your pa to death after he was down."

The shoemaker chuckled. "I think the men in your tales grow mightier each time I hear them. And the women grow prettier."

"After that," the *bayle* said, ignoring the disparaging remark, "Clanoud and Egbeurt often drank together. They had come to truly know the other's worth. They even went off on a Crusade together, as did I."

The *bayle* sneered as he scanned the men around him. "We're all weaklings now." He nodded at Clanoud. "Except for him. Egbeurt went down at Acre under a swarm of Saracens, blood coming out of him like a blessed fountain."

The shoemaker smiled. "You were there?"

The *bayle* stared at him until the shoemaker's insulting smirk disappeared. "Nobody alive was there. They were all wiped out, forty men in all. The prince came to their relief too late, I with him. But I saw the blood and how the bodies lay. I saw what was left of Egbeurt."

The *bayle* took a long drink and wiped his mouth on the sleeve of his tunic. He laughed with ill humor. "Well, it worked out in Sir Jean-Luc's favor, didn't it? Éléonore the widow was a ripe grape for his squeezing. And he made wine with her."

As they marched homeward, Bertwoin said, "I didn't know you and Egbeurt were great friends."

"He was an easy man to like and worth one's company."

"What did you fight over?"

"Éléonore. She might've been your mother if not for Egbeurt laying claim to her. And winning her."

"My mother? A woman who warmed Sir Jean-Luc's bed?"

His father said nothing for nearly fifty steps before clearing his throat. "You judge harshly because you have no more experience than a pup. Priests do likewise, though those who keep mistresses are often a little wiser and more forgiving.

"Éléonore was left a widow, and her kin didn't take care of her. Instead, they took advantage. May God curse them all. She did well for a year or two as the seneschal's mistress. Fed herself and the children who didn't die on her. Most people were glad he took a liking to her. We didn't have to give her charity from what little we had. Many said she was the Church's concern, not ours." He spat. "That's an empty bowl."

"What happened?"

"The usual. After she had his bastard for him, Sir Jean-Luc tired of her. She became the village leper. The ladies on the hill made sure no one at the château helped her. And the women of the villages and towns shunned her. They could forgive Sir Jean-Luc his sin of lust, but not Éléonore's two sins, her being in need and her being beautiful."

Bertwoin thought of Perter's wife, Alesta, Éléonore's daughter. "Now she has Perter for a son-in-law. She seems to have no more luck than Gertrude."

His father hummed agreement. "The seneschal refused to own the bastard Éléonore gave him. And the gossips did the rest. When her half-starved son sickened and died, they said she had left it out in winter weather to catch its death, as Hilario's mother had done with her halfwit boy. But that's just gossips being vicious. Éléonore begged Sir Jean-Luc to help save her boy, his son, but he turned his eyes away from her. She grieved mightily for that lost child."

"Hilario?"

His father smiled up at the white half-moon. "Aye, but the outcome was different. Some folks believe the moon afflicted Hilario's wits after his forgetful mother left her baby outside for an entire night in the cold glare of a fearsome autumn moon. Others tell a more sinister tale. They say Hilario was born disordered, and his weary mother laid her useless son out in the night air, naked so he might catch his death. But what Hilario lacks in sense, he makes up for in rude health. A third of all babies die within their first year, but not the hardy halfwit. He thrived on moonlight and his mother's milk."

"Was Éléonore always a heretic?"

"No. She did tend toward their ways, but it took her awhile before she let her sister persuade her. Maybe that's after the Church turned its back on her when she was in need. So she returned the favor. At least the Good Folk's god will forgive her sins. And Perter, for all his faults, does feed her, though just barely enough to keep her and the family alive."

Clanoud sniffed in contempt. "People judge others harshly for their sins yet are lenient in accepting their own. Hunger is a cruel thing. Éléonore watches her children walk around half-starved while fat Christian burghers in town sit beside warm fires and dine on duck and peacock. No doubt, it makes the Devil laugh."

"Did you help her?"

"I could've done more. I chose not to. The guilt of it lays heavy on me."

Bertwoin remembered Alesta telling him to ask his father why her husband had struck Wilfraed. "Does Perter blame you for not helping her more?"

"I don't know. Who cares how Perter feels?"

"Maybe he cared enough to think he had a good reason to hit Wilfraed."

Clanoud whistled in surprise.

CHAPTER XIX.

Perter decided to reconnoiter the château's kitchen to make sure the larder was empty and that no one was giving it any attention. By now drinks for the honored few who were to sit at the high table were already poured and stood ready on the closet shelves.

He barged through the kitchen's arched doorway and knocked against the slim woman wearing a red scarf as she lugged a black pot to a hearth set in the far wall. He grabbed her thin arm to keep her upright, and she slopped only a bowlful of lentils on the flagstone floor.

Everyone worked with the frantic intensity of disturbed ants and didn't notice him, except for all-seeing Arundel. "You? Out! Clumsy-footed oaf. Out!"

Perter called to the female cook's back as she continued toward a hearth with her heavy pot. "Come back, woman, and sop up what you spilled."

She stared at him in disbelief, then glanced at the chef with the worried look of someone who might have done something wrong.

Seeing that his order had also confused Arundel, one corner of Perter's lip curled upward. "What spilled out on the floor will have more flavor now that it's spiced with dirt the swill Arundel usually serves."

"Out," the chef yelled.

Perter stood a moment, smiling at Arundel to show he would obey him only if he felt generous enough to do so. Then with a grunt, he turned and ambled back into the forecourt.

So now the kitchen was barred to him. Maybe that was honey on his bread. Many had witnessed him leaving and could testify later if need be that he had never gotten past the kitchen's open door.

He sauntered down the front of the long, three-story keep that housed the kitchen. Let Arundel puff up like a pig's bladder. He would soon lose his pompous air. Why did the chef think it his right to order people about like he was a duke? Was a master butcher not the equal of a master chef? Yet Arundel treated him like he was the left side of a carcass, the inferior side, the portions of meat not worthy to be served to those at the high table. Could the snobby chef boast of having known the touch of an angel?

Perter came to a middle door in the keep's stone wall and, seeing no one in the forecourt looking his way, dodged inside the building. A soldier whispered pillow talk to a servant woman in a shadowy corner. After a hurried glance at him, the lovers saw he wasn't important and ignored him.

He hastened through the cool room—glowering ceiling beams, a gaping fireplace, and a stone staircase—and slipped out through the doorway leading into the *Cour du Midi*.

Rows of trestle tables were already set up in the narrow courtyard, but it was still too early to dress them for the coming meal. He stood alone a moment and gloated on his angel-given luck.

Then he scuttled to the larder's small oak door set in the wall on his right and found it barred. Why had he not expected the chef would take precautions? Would Arundel now also have tasters come to his kitchen?

Perter glanced behind him to make certain he was still alone, then peeked through the slit between the larder's door-frame and the oaken door. He saw only darkness. Good, nobody would be inside a dark food closet.

"Give me luck," he whispered to his angel.

He pulled his dagger from its sheath, shoved its blade through the slit underneath the crossbar, and using both hands, worked the bar upwards until it cleared the top of the bracket. He then eased the door open with his shoulder, making sure he kept the crossbar balanced on his knife blade so it didn't clatter to the floor. Once he had pushed halfway inside the larder, he grabbed the bar and swung the door fully open to give himself light.

The room was empty as he had hoped, and the other door leading to the kitchen was closed. His luck had again turned as sweet as ripe berries.

The goblets and tankards for the first drinks at the high table were already filled and lined along a shelf. Perter found the goblet he wanted, the one marked with a diamond, and pulled a tiny clay pot from a hidden pocket sewn onto his tunic under his leather apron. He drew out its stopper and poured the juice into Mistress Millicent's mead. If the chef was using tasters, the mead had probably already been tested.

Perter then peeked out into the *Cour du Midi* and saw no one. So he balanced the crossbar on his knife blade again and backed out of the larder, closing the door until he could drop the bar back into its bracket.

He trotted to the end of the courtyard and slipped past the lovers who were too rapt in their kissing to notice him. Outside in the forecourt, he stretched his back under the

warm autumn sunlight with the smiling satisfaction of a grati-
fied cat. Now no one, not even the master alchemist, could
prove he had poured poison into a goblet stored in a barred
closet. Finding the larder locked had turned out to be another
bit of luck for him.

CHAPTER XX.

As soon as Bertwoin strolled into the château's sunny forecourt that same day, the grinning steward stalked over to him. "You won't be serving today, plowman. Go help the pig-killer instead." He waved at blood-spattered Perter butchering a sow under the fluttering leaves of an elm.

Bertwoin hesitated. Why was the steward reassigning him today? Did it matter? He shrugged, got a leather apron from the kitchen, then ambled back out to the sweating pig-sticker. The smothering stink of fresh blood made him breathe through his mouth.

Perter grunted and pointed his knife at a bucket of scraps and slithery pig intestines he had set aside so the chef could make sausages. When Bertwoin carried it into the hot kitchen deliciously smelling of roasted meat and onions, the chef pointed at two brown-and-white ducks lying on a table and ordered him to pluck them. So Bert-woin dropped onto a stool across from a woman wearing a red headscarf and picked up one of the limp ducks. He glanced around, then asked the young woman where to throw the feathers. She pointed to a stack of oak buckets in a corner. He smiled his thanks and fetched the top one. At least working in the kitchen kept him hidden from Sir Philippe.

He was ripping out handfuls of spiny feathers when Perter shambled into the long room with a bloody ham. He dropped it with a grunt on the stone floor in front of a smoke-blackened hearth.

He then sneered at Bertwoin. "So, shirking your real work by doing women's work in here, are you? I'll see the steward hears of this."

He surveyed the kitchen workers, many of them flushed from tending bubbling pots or snapping fires as they first boiled, then roasted, then braised meat for noble stomachs.

"You can't make some peasants work," Perter announced. He sauntered over to stand behind the young woman in a red headscarf who sat across the table from Bertwoin. Over her head, he growled, "Get back out in the yard where you belong, whelp."

Arundel snarled at Perter, "He stays until I say he goes."

Perter sniffed. "Is that so?" He stomped over to stand nose-to-nose with the master cook. "The steward set him to work with me today."

"You've brought in the ham, butcher. Now get back outside and stop shirking *your* duties." Arundel pointed at Bertwoin. "He stays until *I'm* finished with him."

Eudes paused while shaving slivers of mutton off a leg bone, caught Bertwoin's eye, and made a silly face to show it astonished him that a plowman was so valuable men fought over him like vultures over a sheep's carcass.

Perter ridiculed the cook with a curtsy. "I beg you to forgive my disobedience, milord. I forgot what an honor it is to be in your presence and in your kitchen where bellows boys drop dead and the sons of knights choke on poison." He opened his eyes wide. "Would the plowman not be safer with me? Who knows-"

Arundel smacked the side of the pig-killer's round head with a wooden ladle. Stepping backward out of the chef's reach, Perter shook his head to clear it. He touched the spot where he had been hit above his ear with the tips of his thick fingers. His lips twisted. "Only angels dare tap me, you pinch-faced bastard of a whore." Perter slid his knife from its sheath. "You're about to find yourself in Hell."

Instead of backing away, the chef raised the ladle to strike again. Two cooks holding butcher knives as long as their fore-arms rushed forward to stand on either side of him. One of the chef's defenders was Eudes.

Arundel grinned. "So, come for me now you reeking, shit-eating pig-killer. You'll see a true angel this time, the dark Angel of Death. And I'll see you buried in unhallowed ground, heretic."

"It wouldn't do," drawled an amused voice, "to kill *Visconte* Raimon-Rogièr's chef while the goose still roasts."

Everyone turned toward Sir Reginald, who stood with one regal foot forward as he watched the kitchen drama with practiced boredom. "In the hierarchy of worth, the *visconte* will award more value to his master chef, I think, than to his butcher. Anyone can slit a squealing pig's artery, but few can braise and spice pork with Arundel's flair."

"It's good of you to say so, sir," fawned the cook, whose eyes never left the pig-sticker.

"Well, shall we see if we can't clear away this tiresome dispute so I might obtain some refreshment?" Sir Reginald looked at Arundel for an explanation.

"I need the plowman if I'm to serve the *visconte* and his guests on time today." He flapped a hand at his workers, who were all watching him. "Back to work. *Now*."

"Ah, fighting over your services." Reginald lifted his

eyebrows and nose as he judged Bertwoin. "It must fill you with pride to be so wanted. Maybe you should ask the steward for a higher wage."

Since his parents were profiting from his work more than he was, Bertwoin shrugged. "I'm thinking of becoming a priest and working for wages from on high."

Perter snorted. "You're bound for Hell, piss-pot. Stuffing an ox into a black cassock won't fool either God or the Devil."

Sir Reginald laughed and dipped his head to Perter. "An epigram from a swine killer. Yes, God knows our secrets, as does Satan." He smirked at Bertwoin. "I wonder if I shouldn't teach you a few jests. You can then play the jolly buffoon and entertain us when Itier is dull or eating instead of playing his lute. You are certain to make everyone laugh, even your solemn friend Sir Philippe."

Bertwoin looked pointedly at Perter. "Some think I'm a buffoon already and need not show myself one in public. It might lessen my wages. And it might lose me work. People will doubt a prancing fool can plow a straight furrow for them."

Perter grunted. "Playing the fool is a tailor's fit for you. It's your natural state."

"As you wish," Sir Reginald said to Bertwoin, "though, it is a pity. You seem to have the wit for it. And it takes true wit to play a fool if you are not one. But now to the problem at hand. To keep peace in the kitchen, plowman, hurry and finish plucking the poultry. Then you will serve me today. I have the honor of sitting at the head table."

Bertwoin flinched. What game did this knight mean to play?

"Sir," Bertwoin said, "you will find me unpracticed and unlearned in the ways of serving. You might find me offering you meat reserved for some other guest or your bread following your dessert."

"Then you will add the diverting spice of novelty to our banquet. You may play the fool yet." Sir Reginald looked with distaste at Bertwoin's soiled leather apron and a smear of blood on the sleeve of his tunic. "When you finish here, see my squire. I will tell him to outfit you so you may wear the blue-and-white livery of my family and serve me with distinction."

Perter harrumphed. "You are asking a leper to serve you, sir."

"Sir Philippe did not fear contagion. So why should I?" Sir Reginald rubbed his hands together. "I think, though, that Sir Philippe will chafe indeed to see the plowman so raised in honor that he serves at the high table."

Bertwoin realized the hostage knight was using him to tweak his enemy's nose, but he needed this ally inside the château.

"Well," Bertwoin said, "if nothing else, sir, you shall have the amusement of seeing me spill soup on Lady Trencavel's head and seeing me kicked from one end of the long court-yard to the other."

Delighted by the idea, Perter clapped his hands.

WEARING SIR REGINALD'S BLUE-AND-WHITE LIVERY, Bertwoin surveyed the *Cour du Midi*. The white stripes in the *visconte's* linen tablecloths gleamed in the sun like purity itself. Did the red stripes stand for blood?

Servants had already laid out silver trenchers and clay bowls and goblets and cups. Four sets of ornate, pewter salt bowls also decorated the head table. Bertwoin assumed Sir

Philippe was important enough to have crushed salt at his table too.

After the chamberlain blared the brass horn to invite the château's noble residents and guests to a sumptuous meal, Bertwoin carried weighty pewter and silver platters of food handed to him by the head butler to the high table. He watched the other servers and followed their manners and actions.

Itier thrummed his lute as he sang in a clear voice of wistful love or in more guttural tones of heroic deeds. Bertwoin heard the tale of Roland's death while protecting Charlemagne's army from ambush and wondered if Roland the boar would guard Flowia's rear with such heroic loyalty.

Between songs, Itier bantered with guests to amuse those at the high table. He noticed Bertwoin and shouted, "You carry that platter with such solemn dignity, peasant, I think you bring us the boar's head for a centerpiece."

"All food should be served with dignity, sir."

"Bring us a boar's head, and if the kitchen has none on hand, why then we may use your head. What think you of that?"

"I think you must dance first and please noble *Visconte* Raimon-Rogièr before you may ask for my head on a platter."

Bertwoin glanced at the *visconte* to see if he had taken offense at being compared to Herod and saw him laugh. Itier strummed a resounding chord on his lute to show appreciation for Bertwoin's allusion. The abbot frowned with disapproval.

"What think you, Abbot Jehan?" Itier asked. "Do we have here a rustic Saint John the Baptist?"

"It is impertinent to say so."

Turning back to Bertwoin, Itier said, "You'll never see me dance, peasant. And the noble *visconte* would hand out no prize to watch you dance like a man hopping across furrows. We would have to bring in a mule to accompany you."

A little piqued by Itier's emphasizing his low-born status, Bertwoin hesitated, thought a moment, then copied Flowia's rhyming speech.

> "If given the head of a lutist
> I will contrive to do my best
> so my peasant clumsiness
> might amuse the distinguished guests."

"That you shall never have, peasant," Itier snapped.

A wine-happy knight shouted from one of the back tables, "Let the bear dance."

"My fee is the head of Itier the lutist," Bertwoin reminded him.

"I'll remove Itier's head for you if need be," the man shouted back.

"Will you not accept the head of a boar instead of a troubadour's head?" Sir Reginald called out as if Bertwoin were far away from him. "We wish to see you dance. And there's little difference between the two heads, is there not?"

"But, sir," Bertwoin answered, "it is the boar's head that brings honor to the table."

Noble-born Itier was a favorite with *Viscontesse* Agnes, so she refrained from laughing at the insult. Some of the men below the salt pounded their tables with the flat of their hands in appreciation of Bertwoin's jibe.

Visconte Raimon-Rogièr drawled, "I think a boar's head glazed is more palatable than Itier's head dazed."

Sir Reginald caught Bertwoin's eye and twitched his head toward the larder. It was time for retreat. Bertwoin, relieved, escaped to the food closet as if to fetch a dish there. After that, he kept as much in the background as possible, and no one seemed to notice him except Itier and Sir Philippe.

He had just set a blancmange colored green with mint and other herbs on a side serving table, when Mistress Millicent, Sir Jean-Luc's thirteen-year-old daughter, vomited. Sir Reginald, who sat beside her, scooted his chair back so as not to soil his silk tunic.

"No," the *viscontesse* screamed.

The abbot proclaimed, "God has cursed this château."

"This only happens," the young *visconte* snapped, "when you sit as a guest here."

Mistress Millicent shoved her chair back and stood, her expression dazed with disbelief. She stared with distempered sight down the long courtyard and complained, "It is not proper for monks to wear yellow."

Sir Jean-Luc pleaded, "No. Please no. Not my lambkin too."

She tottered. Bertwoin stepped forward to steady her, but she collapsed at his feet before he could catch her. He grabbed a folded tablecloth off a side table and spread it over her. The butler and everyone at the high table stared at him in disbelief.

"Help me," Bertwoin shouted to the butler. "We must carry her to a bedroom and lay her in the dark."

The butler stared at him, stupefied by the idea of a peasant seizing control of an emergency and daring to give him an order.

"Now," Bertwoin shouted.

Sir Reginald darted forward and stooped to grab Millicent's delicate ankles under the white linen sheet. Bertwoin slid his hands under her armpits, and they lifted her with the tablecloth still on her. Bertwoin was surprised how little she weighed, no more than a sheaf of wheat.

He told the seneschal, "Sir, we need charcoal crushed in

water and a second drink of mustard seed also ground in water."

Sir Jean-Luc turned to the butler and shouted, "Make it so."

He then led them toward his daughter's bedroom. On the way, Mistress Millicent woke and began babbling and thrashing about. They laid her on her four-poster bed and drew its heavy brocaded curtains closed to darken the interior. The *viscontesse* and Hytha rushed into the room.

Sir Reginald bowed to them, then left the room to the women. The *viscontesse* leaned partly inside the curtain and grabbed Mistress Millicent's hand and held it against her forehead, sobbing.

Bertwoin told Hytha, "She must drink the charcoal in water and later the mustard in water. I will run to fetch Flowia."

"Go!" she told him. "I will see to what needs to be done here."

Bertwoin hurried back to the *Cour du Midi*, which he found empty except for Sir Reginald, who sat alone in the *visconte's* chair at the high table. "Has she died?"

"Not yet, sir." He thought of Hytha and how strong women, unlike the paralyzed butler, were more valuable than knights in some emergencies. "And God willing, she won't."

"Will this charcoal cure of yours save her, do you think?"

"If not, sir, I will have to flee. If she dies, they will only remember my impertinence and will blame me for not keeping her alive."

Bertwoin picked a clean tablecloth off a side table, unfolded it, then bundled Mistress Millicent's vomit-smelling dishes in it.

Sir Reginald hummed in sympathy. "It was brave of you to take on the duty of saving her."

"Or stupid," Bertwoin told the knight hostage. "It took no courage, sir. I did it without thought."

Reginald waved a hand at Mistress Millicent's empty place at the high table. "I see. If you are forced to flee, the *visconte's* silver and pewter may buy you a lusty ram and several ewes so you can set up as a fugitive shepherd."

"I do not take these for gain, sir. I think the master alchemist will think it important for him to study the food on these plates and the mead in her goblet."

Reginald nodded. "Yes. Her being stricken like her brother argues for another poisoning. And she so recently betrothed to some beardless prince in Aragon." He stared a moment at the *visconte's* dessert plate and sighed. "In future, I think I shall decline to eat at the high table."

He waved Bertwoin away. "Run your errand, plowman. Save our fair damsel. Oh, and if you must flee, come to me by night first. I will find you a position in my father's kingdom."

Bertwoin had an uncle who had fled to the Pyrenees after blinding a trader during a brawl at a fair. He was a *chef de cabane*, the leader of a group of shepherds, and would take him in. But this offer to work for Sir Reginald's family was tempting. Could he work there as a plowman? A knot formed in his throat. What would he do about Flowia?

"Thank you, sir," he said.

"Not at all. It is for my pleasure, not yours. You are quick-witted and also have the delightful habit of being entertaining."

WHEN BERTWOIN BURST INTO THE CANDLELIT WORKSHOP, he found the master hunched over a small table, hammering a pattern into a silver plate, and Flowia working beside the hearth set in one wall. Both were startled rigid for a moment.

He told them the poisoner had struck down Mistress Millicent, then lifted the tablecloth bulging with clanking metal. "I brought her dishes."

"What signs did she display?" the alchemist asked.

"The same as those her brother showed, master." Bertwoin turned to Flowia. "I told them to give Mistress Millicent charcoal in water, then to crush mustard seed in water for her, as you told me to do."

Flowia lifted her hands toward the low ceiling, "*Deo Gratias.*"

"You were quick as a fox, young man," the master praised.

Bertwoin stood a little straighter. "I told them I would bring Flowia."

Her eyes wide with alarm, she told the alchemist, "But surely they will send for Brother Theodoric so he can tend to her while they fetch a doctor."

"It's me they'll blame if she dies," Bertwoin said, "not you. The seneschal ordered the charcoal to be given to his daughter on *my* word. Hytha said she would see to the dose of mustard seed. You need to be there to supervise."

"They'll not let me nurse her."

Bertwoin wanted Flowia there to make the cure he had ordered work, not Brother Theodoric, a goodly monk, but also one who would take the credit if Mistress Millicent lived but pass the blame on to him if she died. "Hytha expects you and will see to it that you are allowed into the bedchamber."

"Escort her to the château," the master told Bertwoin, settling the argument. "If Flowia looks to remain there throughout the afternoon and night, return here." He waved at the linen tablecloth and dishes Bertwoin held. "I have tests to perform, and your assistance will hasten my work."

"Did she eat mustard during the meal?" Flowia asked.

"Yes, everyone does. They eat great quantities of it."

"That may be to her advantage."

"Is it not the same poison as last time?" Bertwoin asked.

"Probably," the alchemist said, "but I must determine for certain that it was belladonna. And if I can determine the vehicle used for the poison, whether it was mead or bread or meat, we might begin to learn the murderer's pattern. Now go. I must work quickly before I am summoned to the château. Bring me back news of the seneschal's daughter. And may it lift our spirits."

CHAPTER XXI.

As Bertwoin had predicted, Hytha had spoken to the *viscontesse* and seneschal and convinced them that Flowia must nurse Mistress Millicent in her bedchamber until the physician arrived. They were, in fact, restless with impatience for her arrival. Black-robed Brother Theodoric, whose medicinal herb garden, like Flowia's, was renowned throughout the diocese, was reassured to see her already treating the patient when he rushed in from the abbey.

Bertwoin's spirit danced above the clouds when he learned that Mistress Millicent still lived. Now that she was under the healing care of both Flowia and Brother Theodoric, her chances of surviving to marry her beardless prince were favorable. And after the physician arrived, Sir Jean-Luc might think of ordering her wedding dress.

Before rushing back to help the alchemist with his work, Bertwoin decided to talk with sly Arundel. Why not? He was still inside the château, and he thought the master would forgive him for trying to learn something that might help them catch this killer before he struck again.

The kitchen's smell of fried meat and onions reminded him of the warm comfort of his household, though unlike here, his *maman's* home cooking didn't poison people.

Arundel sat beside the first hearth, basting a long pork loin that roasted on a spit. The fire under it hissed as grease dripped into it. Neither sickness nor death prevented the thirty or so people residing in the château from expecting supper. But would they want to eat food from the château's deadly kitchen?

Without rising, the chef mocked him with a slight bow. "Here is a plowman who knows the secrets of charcoal and mustard. You honor my kitchen. Have you come to sample our dishes and find the poison?"

A young apprentice cook laughed. The other workers smiled, except for Eudes, who kept his expression neutral.

Bertwoin leaned against the main table in the center of the room. Why did Arundel want to hinder the solving of this crime? "Find what poison?" he asked the chef. "I'm sure the fishes in the Aude now feast on those leftovers."

"Take care, young pup. Or I will have you kicked out of my kitchen."

Would Eudes help hustle him outside? "I met Béatrice waiting in the forecourt with her family," he told Arundel. "She told me no scraps from this feast were given to them."

"Go away, Ox. Let the *bayle* do his duty and find this killer. You're a juggler who will drop all of the colored balls. You lack the practiced skill for this."

"The master sent me." The alchemist *had* told him to escort Flowia back to the château. "This morning, did anyone enter your kitchen who had no real business here?"

Arundel laughed. "Who didn't, plowman?" The chef glanced at a stocky grill cook named Bernard. "Many shorten their route to the *Cour du Midi* by trespassing through my busy kitchen. Often, I have to post Bernard at the door to keep people out. And you, plowman, you were in here too, same as when the seneschal's son died. Tell your master alchemist that."

"Did Tolarto come in?" Bertwoin suffered a slight disgust with himself. He was flailing around like a fish trying to throw itself off a hook.

The chef waved away the silly accusation. "Who remembers? If he had a delivery, he probably did. If for no other reason than to pinch-poach a bite or two off our tables."

Bertwoin nodded. "So I am to tell the master that the poisoner is someone you see in your kitchen every day and don't notice?" He remembered hearing a server mention a quarrel. "Wasn't there an argument in your kitchen before the meal?"

"Ah, that. It *was* odd. Not like Sir Reginald at all. He shoved Bernard aside and burst into my kitchen. He stormed about in a ripe rage. Something to do with Sir Philippe. To cool his ire, he demanded bread soaked in wine; and when it was not given to him before he could snap his fingers, he became bilious. Overturned a pot of pea soup and had to be escorted out, even if he is a knight. Not like him. You didn't hear of this?" the chef asked as though only simpletons or the deaf didn't know everything that happened in his all-important kitchen.

"I only heard some talk of an argument and took little heed of it. And it's not surprising that Sir Philippe is the cause. He could make an angel curse."

"Still it was odd. Sir Reginald knows that my kitchen is the heart and soul of the château. He appreciates how important our work is."

"So Sir Reginald visits the kitchen often?"

"Usually once or twice a day. He comes in person instead of sending a servant. He is most particular about his victuals and drink."

Like Master Servay, Bertwoin thought. "Any idea what Sir Philippe had done to make Sir Reginald so peevish?"

The chef shrugged. "A lover's spat, I would think. Troubadours sing of emerald and sard, but gallantry and wooing can be strenuous on young knights. Their lady loves are not always kind. She...well it is no business of mine."

Bertwoin didn't ask what the chef meant by "emerald and sard" because he didn't want to seem ignorant. He would ask Flowia later about this mysterious "sard."

He had heard that Sir Reginald, like Sir Philippe, paid homage to beautiful Lady Trencavel though she was only thirteen years old. It was said she enjoyed his attention, and what lady wouldn't? Sir Reginald was blond and handsome. Women talked of his peacock-blue eyes, or so Flowia had told him. The hostage knight sang almost as well as Itier, and though imperious like all nobility, he had nice manners. Many, though, thought him frivolous and too much given to humor. He was also foreign.

Bertwoin frowned as he remembered first seeing Sir Reginald in Arundel's kitchen. "Just after the bellows boy died, Sir Reginald was also part of a disturbance in here. He, Hytha, and Sir Philippe argued. The two knights seemed only a few words away from brawling."

Arundel thrust out his chest. "As I said, the kitchen is the château's beating heart. It's a room of passion. So we have our little spats. Now let me prepare this roast in peace. The ladies and lords will not accept delay or forgive me for a badly cooked meal. Give the master my best." He made the sign of the cross over the top of his apron.

As many other people did, Arundel believed that, like witches, the master heard whatever was said about him. Blessing his name while making the sign of the cross was thought to appease him. Not even the *visconte* could boast of having such superstitious power over his people.

CHAPTER XXII

Two days later, Flowia again came to Bertwoin's house to fetch him. They were to meet the master in Montredon. As they ambled down the path, she teased him by telling him that Tisbe had found something surprisingly morbid in her tavern, but Flowia refused to name it.

"I had something to tell you too," he said, his tone making it clear that he wasn't going to share it with her before she told him her news.

She shrugged but stopped and kissed his cheek to bribe him into confessing his secret.

"It's in the forest not far from here," he said. "I need to show it to you."

She pealed a tiny laugh, paused a second to think, then told him, "A newly born lamb/that's not what I am/to be led astray/by a lusty wolf today." She bowed her head and smiled up at him. "The master waits for us, and this business cannot be delayed."

She continued to give him hints as they walked to

Montredon, but he feigned disinterest in her taunting riddles. Her eyes lost the luster of mischief, and her expression settled into one of resigned disappointment. To please her, he made a few guesses, and she patted his shoulder, accepting his willingness to indulge her teasing.

The alchemist sat alone at one of Tisbe's four tables, stroking his white beard and staring down into a bowl as if its reflective surface might show him a vision. The other three tables were packed with people waiting to witness an act of magic. The master looked as gravely impassive and timeless as a mountain.

He greeted Bertwoin as they sat down at his table, then jerked his chin at the ever-alert Tisbe to signal he wanted drinks for his two guests.

"Well, plowman, what do you think of our find?"

Bertwoin gave Flowia an accusatory glance. "I have not yet learned of it."

Flowia sniffed and told the master, "I thought it best for *you* to tell him."

"Did you?" the alchemist asked, clearly not understanding why. "Well, one of Tisbe's two tenants began to notice a foul smell in her room, and some of her customers complained about it. When the girl searched for the source of this stink, she noticed flies swarming near her clothes chest. She had dug a cache under it. She found Master Servay's rotting head stuffed in the hole."

"What?" Bertwoin blurted out. "Who else knew of her hiding place? How did anyone put it there without the girl seeing them? And how—?"

The master raised a bony hand to stop his outburst. For a moment, there was silence, and Bertwoin noticed that all of the people sitting at the other three tables leaned forward, some with their ear turned toward them.

The master hummed. "Good questions that will require

further investigation and further thought. I do hope that finding this head will provide a modicum of solace to Sir Jean-Luc. Though he doesn't yet have his son's body, he now has the head and can bury it in hallowed ground."

"The soul is seated in the head," a roofer's wife called from one of the other tables.

The alchemist half bowed to her. "I'll not argue against that, mistress."

The roofer's wife sat as proud as a hen hatching eggs.

"Fortunately," the master said, "after finding the head, Tisbe notified me first." He nodded his thanks to her as she stood in her doorway, ready to refill anyone's empty bowl or tankard. "So I was able to examine the skull before the *bayle* removed it."

"Thank you, *bayle*," Bertwoin whispered. After a few days, a corpse was at its ripest, and he was glad the decaying head was now gone.

The alchemist agreed with a nod. "Not a pleasant task, I assure you. Anyway, Aimée also-"

"Aimée?" Bertwoin asked.

"Yes, Tisbe's tenant, the one whose room was desecrated. I was able to talk with Aimée before the *bayle* took her for questioning."

Flowia praised Bertwoin by patting his forearm. "Not knowing her name does you credit, Bertwoin."

He thought it odd that she would say this since her mother had been a prostitute. But maybe she meant it showed he loved only her.

A woman guffawed, honking like an alarmed goose. A carter called out, "Master, if you need a second virgin, there he is sitting across from you."

Laughter rippled around the other tables. Flowia and Bertwoin avoided looking at each other.

The alchemist smiled at the carter, then continued, "So

she found the head grinning up at her from her cache. She had secreted deniers in the hole, and of course, these were missing. The murderer must have exalted over his unexpected luck."

"And you were able to identify who once wore that head without trouble?" Bertwoin asked.

"Ah well, the skin *had* already slipped. The face appeared to have melted, and maggots had feasted like kings and left only a pulp of rotting flesh, but the *bayle* confirmed my belief that the skull belonged to Master Servay. Its foremost left tooth was chipped. The seneschal's son put his hand in front of his mouth often to hide this particular defect. He believed it marred his handsomeness."

"But why leave the head here?" Flowia asked.

"At least we now know," the roofer's wife called to them, "if it wasn't a cruel man who stuffed that head in that hole, it was a true demon." She scanned those at her table to see if the others agreed with her before she said with smug assurance, "No angel carried that boy's soul off to heaven."

The alchemist whispered, "That one is sharper than a splinter of glass."

"Angels are welcome here," Tisbe told the roofer's wife as she set a tankard in front of a carpenter with one ear missing. People laughed, and some of them glanced toward the rooms where her two tenants worked. Tisbe looked at the master, silently questioning whether he wanted more to drink. He shook his head and got out his coin purse.

"Come," he said to Flowia and Bertwoin, "I have learned all I can here. We'll discuss what Aimée told me as we walk back to the cottage."

But the alchemist didn't speak as he led them out of Montredon and across the wooden bridge over the Aude where it began its curve around the village like a natural moat. They ambled along the river's bank, their measured thoughts keeping pace with their steps.

Finally, the alchemist shook his head as if coming awake and adjusted his red hat. "Aimée had little to tell me and seemed more distraught over finding her coins stolen than she did in finding a rotting skull hidden in her room. She believed she alone knew she had a cache, and she had never met Master Servay.

"As to Tisbe, well, she told me a rat couldn't slip into her household without her knowing of it. But she does have many visitors." The alchemist hummed laughter. "And she believes she can turn this scandal from rotting flesh into shiny silver. She says folks will gossip about her tavern and come like pilgrims to see the place for themselves. Tisbe is ordering extra ale to augment what she brews herself."

"So," Flowia said, "if we assume the killer planted the head, then we can assume he is one of us, a peasant or trades-man. A nobleman coming to Montredon to drink at Tisbe's would be remembered. And most clerics frequent the taverns in the towns closer to the citadel."

"So does this killer come to Tisbe's tavern often?" Bert-woin asked.

"Maybe." Flowia pursed her lips. "Though carrying a stinking head was sure to draw unwanted attention. How did he do it?"

"What if the killer is taunting the *bayle?*" Bertwoin asked. "It *is* the old crusader's place of business when he's not in the château."

"Perhaps," the master said. "Or is the killer drawing our attention to some scandal attached to Master Servay? Why a prostitute's room? Or if you are correct," he said to Bertwoin, "does the *bayle* visit Aimée?"

Bertwoin perked up at a thought. "Ah, no one is at the

tavern on Sunday mornings. Tisbe and everyone who works for her go to mass."

Flowia clapped her hands. "Well said, Bertwoin."

"Yes," the alchemist agreed. "Now we know when the rat might have slipped into the tavern and left behind his spiteful gift."

They quieted as they neared the uprooted willow where Janus the fisherman had found the woodcutter's daughter floating face down in the river with the bottom of her chemise burnt and her feet blistered by fire. Bertwoin made the sign of the cross in remembrance of young Emeline, then glanced at Flowia, who looked grim. Yes, that murderer gave her nightmares.

"Na Thea told me two people now claim they saw poor Emeline's ghost wandering near here," Flowia said.

The master grumbled, "Doubtless someone will soon see a headless corpse wandering the corridors of the château."

Flowia gave Bertwoin a flattering look of praise. "We are fortunate Master Servay's sister didn't join him."

The master nodded. "Yes, Bertwoin acted with alacrity. And I'm certain bringing you," he said to Flowia, "to the château so quickly also helped prevent her death."

Under the pleasant weight of his compliment, Flowia glided along, smiling at the ground.

Bertwoin asked, "So do we know how she was poisoned?"

"Yes," Flowia said. "Death cherries, the same poison that killed her brother, tainted the residue left in her goblet. Another pat on the back goes to you for bringing us her dishes."

"Have you returned them to the château?"

Flowia reared back and looked up at him in shocked surprise. "Why ever would we do so?/We decided to keep them as a souvenir/and spare the seneschal the woe/of remembering that his daughter's death was near." She waggled her head, smiling. "Besides, they were freely brought to us."

Bertwoin laughed. "Free, maiden? I think not. The price of your keeping them is me losing a hand or being hung as a thief."

"Oh, a cheap price then, and one we are willing to pay."

CHAPTER XXIII.

erter hid in a row of plane trees bordering a horse pasture until he saw the squire, a teenager named Gidie, carry a wooden bucket of oats to a courser belonging to Sir Philippe. The pig-killer grunted and strolled into sight, the late autumn Tramontane wind flattening his cloak against his body.

The squire set the bucket on the ground before the horse, and it began to feed. Gidie then saw the butcher approaching him and frowned with undisguised annoyance. Perter smiled to reassure him. The horse's brown eyes studied him a moment before it flicked its ears and returned to eating oats from the bucket.

Perter swaggered up and examined the courser. "Nice horse."

The white stallion looked hot-blooded, sturdily built yet agile enough for both hunting and war, and the coming of winter had already turned its coat shaggy. Its mane rippled in the unruly wind as if alive.

"What are you doing here, butcher? Don't you have work in the château?"

Perter grunted. Oh yes, this ass-wipe was training up well. He'd soon be as haughty as the knight he served. Perter yawned, taking his time to irritate the boy. "I have news your knight will wish to hear."

One side of Gidie's mouth curled upward dismissively, yet he also perked up with interest. "What could you know that he doesn't?"

"I know that the plowman told the steward that Sir Philippe failed to do his duty when he didn't protect Master Servay's life and later when he let the body be stolen."

Gidie sneered. "A peasant's insult?" He flipped his hand in disdain, and the horse raised its head at the sudden movement. "My knight, butcher, already knows this."

Perter ducked his head slightly to suggest a bow of respect. "He also says Sir Philippe is a coward who pays money so he doesn't have to fight."

"You would do well to watch your tongue, churl."

"And you would do well, pustule, to put some wit inside your empty head."

The squire was too startled to speak and stared at him with his mouth open.

Pleased at his insult's effect, Perter growled, "I'm not the one who insulted your knight, squire. I only repeat what the plowman tells everyone. Maybe I should tell this to Sir Philippe himself instead of his turd-brained servant. He knows enough to listen to words that will profit him."

Gidie balled his hands into fists and stepped closer. They were of equal height, but though the squire's forearms were muscular from training with a heavy sword, the butcher's forearms were twice their size.

"If you come at me, pup, I'll snap your neck like a piece of kindling. Your wrestling throws won't work on me."

When Gidie touched his dagger's handle, Perter slipped a

long butcher knife out from under his leather belt. "I'm good at cutting up piglets, pustule."

The squire jerked his fingers off his dagger. He started to walk away, but Perter stepped in front of him.

Gidie swallowed and said, "My ears are unstopped."

"Good. Know this, when the plowman served Sir Philippe at table, he spat in his drink and also smeared dog shit from the floor on the underside of the meat he served him."

The squire's hands again curled into fists.

"And I, myself," said Perter, "came upon the plowman without warning and saw him pour something into Mistress Millicent's mead before she fell into a fit."

The squire's eyes lit up, then dulled with doubt. "Yet he's the one who saved her life."

Perter shook his head in pity. Gidie had the makings of a brawny warrior when he ripened to full manhood, but even a fierce ram only has the brain of a sheep.

"That's because he knew exactly what poison he had given her and so knew the remedy. And now the plowman sits in good regard with the *visconte* and his seneschal. Can Sir Philippe say the same? He annoyed *Visconte* Raimon-Rogièr at the feast while the wily plowman was serving your knight spit and shit."

Gidie said, frowning, "Why have you not told anyone about the plowman poisoning the mead before now?"

"I just told you."

Perter turned abruptly and strode away, whistling. The squire would tell his knight what he had heard. He was sure of that. And once Sir Philippe heard how Clanoud's son had slandered him and had mistreated him at the feast, he was sure to swoop down on the simple plowman.

CHAPTER XXIV.

B ertwoin was sitting on a stool, cutting a strap of horse leather for a plow harness, when Sir Philippe rode into the front yard on a white palfrey with two squires behind him on roan rouncies. Outraged geese honked and flapped their wings as they dodged the horses' legs. Bertwoin had no wings to spread, but inwardly he felt as the geese did.

Though his heartbeat quickened, he rose with deliberate calm and stood with his arms folded over his chest. The squire named Gidie urged his horse closer. Sir Philippe had stopped farther back as if coming too close might contaminate him. He scanned the farm, his disdainful sneer an insult, then spat on the hard-packed dirt. "So this is your smutty den, peasant."

Clanoud strode out of the barn, carrying a hoe and hayfork. He handed the hoe to Bertwoin, then swaggered over to where Sir Philippe sat on the palfrey that was worth as much as their farm.

Bertwoin relaxed a bit when he noticed that the knight and his squires were armed only with daggers. His father facing Sir Philippe with a hayfork was a serious threat, though the knight pretended not to notice him.

Gidie said, "It smells like shit here."

"It didn't until you rode in," Bertwoin said.

The squire stared down at Bertwoin with disbelief, his mouth slightly open. He glanced at Sir Philippe, then back at Bertwoin. "We already know you're surly and have a ready tongue, peasant. You need not prove it to us. We also know of your disrespect for my knight. Someone saw you spit in his cup before you filled it with ale. The person also saw you rub dog shit on the meat you served my knight. You're too stupid even to hide your crimes."

Bertwoin relaxed further so his muscles wouldn't be tight if he had to move swiftly.

Gidie waited for an answer, and when he got none, he said, "You were overheard insulting Sir Philippe, calling him a false knight, a coward." Again he waited for an answer and received none. "Well, yokel, not so ready to use your tongue now, are you?"

Bertwoin slicked a hand along the hoe's long, smooth handle. "Why should I answer you? You've come to start a quarrel whether the charge is true or not. Your ears ring so loud with lies, you won't hear the truth."

Gidie's lips curled with contempt. "The *visconte's* charity sometimes exceeds his reason. He sometimes allows dunces to serve at his feasts. He doesn't know yet of your crime, but he will have you punished when he learns of it."

"Only if there's proof," Clanoud growled. "And there'll be no punishment here and now."

Bertwoin knew his father intended to take care of Sir Philippe if it came to a fight. He and his hoe would have to contend with the two squires.

Gidie half turned in his saddle and snarled to Clanoud,

"Shit-eating vermin do not give orders to their betters. Why ever does the *visconte* not whip you all?"

"Because we produce geese and eggs and loaves of bread for his tables," Bertwoin answered. It was time to provoke the attack. "Knights do little but dine and play at fighting." He looked with scorn at Sir Philippe. "And your knight's grandeur is in his purse, not his arms."

During a recent border dispute between the *visconte* and a neighboring baron, Sir Philippe had paid scutage, a fee *Visconte* Raimon-Rogièr used to hire soldiers to replace Philippe, who didn't fight.

"And what good are you?" Bertwoin said directly to Gidie. "You train, you fawn over your knight, you eat, you shit, and you sleep softer than most."

Bertwoin readied for the squire's attack. Such an insult to Sir Philippe's honor could not go unpunished, which was why Bertwoin had said it. It was better to fight Sir Philippe and his squires here with his father backing him than to be caught alone later on the road or in town.

"Well," Gidie muttered, "it seems the cur must be brought to heel."

He raised his whip and spurred his horse forward. Bertwoin took half a step toward the rouncy instead of retreating and slapped the horse's soft nose. It balked.

Bertwoin leaped sideways and speared the squire in the stomach with his hoe. Doubled-over, Gidie tumbled out of his saddle and landed on his back, the breath blown from his lungs.

Sir Philippe yawned and smirked at Clanoud, who stood with the tines of his deadly hayfork slanted upward toward the knight's belly.

The second squire spurred his horse forward, but Gidie's vexed roan stepped in the way. Bertwoin jumped to one side as the second squire fought to bring his agitated horse under control. Bertwoin jabbed the hoe's flat blade against the squire's chest and unhorsed him. The squire landed on his feet but fell forward on his knees and palms. Quick as a terrier, he leaped up and snicked out his dagger.

Bertwoin chopped the squire's hand with the hoe's cutting edge. The boy yelped and dropped his dagger. He cradled his injured hand against his chest and wheezed as if huffing would lessen the pain. Blood began seeping through the fingers of the hand he held over the injury.

Sir Philippe shook his head at the defeat of his squires by peasants and, too proud to fight a peasant himself, turned his excellent palfrey and rode out of the yard.

Clanoud's face twisted with hard contempt as he watched Sir Philippe ride away. "Not one to stand beside you once you've fallen, is he?" He jerked his chin at the two squires and told Bertwoin, "Get their knives."

When the squires were again on their feet, Clanoud told Bertwoin, "If we just let them ride away, they might not take the lesson to heart. Maybe we should beat them awhile and let them explain to their fellows why their faces are yellow and blue."

"They were just following orders."

"Ever the generous son," his father said. He sneered at the squires. "Get gone and don't ever come back unless you want your heads broken."

As they watched the squires ride away, Clanoud muttered, "All the money spent on those idiots, yet they're not worth horse drool. They'll be lucky to remain squires to Sir Philippe or any other knight once this gets known." He slapped his thigh. "Bested by peasants."

"Maybe Sir Philippe won't tell anyone," Bertwoin said. "It does him no honor either. And they'U not brag about today."

Clanoud rolled his shoulders, enlivened by the skirmish even though he hadn't taken part in it. "You think I won't tell everybody? If we don't shame them and drive them out of the domain, they'll take revenge on you. Getting rid of them is our only hope. Until we do, watch your step when you're working at the château. And from now on, keep your face hole shut."

Bertwoin almost asked, *You mean like you do*? But he decided to take his father's advice and keep his mouth closed.

CHAPTER XXV

Bertwoin was marching toward the indomitable citadel when he saw Flowia on the wooden bridge, staring down at the sluggish Aude as it basked in the morning sunlight. He trotted to her but didn't kiss her, though he longed to do so. The bridge was busy with people, many carrying supplies to the citadel and its down-slope towns.

"Come," she said, "the master has need of your strong legs today."

"But I'm on my way to work at the château."

"Already I have spoken to the steward/told him the master needs his ox today/this the steward did not controvert/so you earn no pay this day." She turned and glided toward the master's cottage.

"Good then," Bertwoin said. "You relieve me of maybe having to serve meat at Sir Philippe's table. He means to take revenge on me." He told her of the knight's visit to their farm.

"We will need to speak with the master about this," she

said. "Sir Philippe is a formidable enemy. And what's more, he's a favorite with both the *viscontesse* and the seneschal."

He gave her a boyish look of hope. "Are we going through the woods?"

"That would delay our arrival. The master is waiting for me to bring you."

"But he won't know how long you had to wait for me at the bridge."

He took her hand and turned off the main road onto an empty path that eventually led to the cottage.

"Is this a shorter route?" she teased.

"No, but the way is much more pleasant," he said with a cooing lilt.

In the forest, a green Eden vibrant with life yet also comfortingly still, they quickly found a secluded place, a lover's nest hidden behind the fallen, lichen-encrusted trunk of an elm. There she faced him and reached up to caress his cheek. He gently clasped her hand, brought it to his mouth, and kissed her wrist. She moved against him, fitting herself to him. He inhaled deeply, savoring the rosemary scent in her hair. She put her ear against his chest as if to listen to his heartbeat, which now raced with delicious arousal.

"We must not tarry," she murmured.

He whisper-kissed her silky eyebrows, her eyelids, then brush-kissed her lips, teasing her, promising her gentle love. Flowia moaned with desire and clasped her to him, her eyes closed, her yearning expression angelic.

His hands explored her womanly body, slowly, with adoration. When he nuzzled her ear, she shuddered as his beard tickled across her neck like butterfly wings. He laid her down on the luxuriant moss.

Bertwoin surrendered to a wisdom known only to the body. Sexual bliss was all-powerful and as radiant in him as the sun. Flowia eclipsed the leafy world around them and became his entire universe.

Afterward, he relaxed into a delicious malaise and tossed his head like a high-spirited stallion.

"Are you all right?" he whispered huskily, panting. He pressed her against his body and wished he knew how to make her understand how precious she was to him. But he knew of no words strong enough.

Flowia patted his neck. Did she know how he felt?

CHAPTER XXVI

Sometimes a painful disease inflamed one or both of the master's large toes, causing him to hobble like a lame pilgrim in search of a divine cure. When he was thus afflicted, Flowia cooked nettle soup for him; and if they were in season, she fed him ripe cherries. He also drank less wine and no ale during these attacks and rested his feet until his swollen, red toes shrank back to normal size and lost their unnatural heat. The local priest assured the master that this ailment was sent as punishment for his sins.

The disease had again lamed him at a time when he needed to visit Alesta's mother, the beautiful Éléonore who was renowned for her perfect skin and notorious for her disastrous affair with Sir Jean-Luc. So Flowia had suggested that Bertwoin be the ox for their handcart, and as he pulled the master in it to Éléonore's house, she marched along beside them, carrying a hemp sack filled with a joint of roast pork. Charity was more welcome than any saint at Éléonore's house.

"Flowia said you wanted to question Éléonore about the

murders," Bertwoin said over his shoulder to the alchemist. "Do you really think she knows anything?"

"She lived inside the château for some time and knows much about its ways. But what is valuable about her is that her tongue isn't tied by loyalty. Just the opposite, in fact."

Flowia explained, "Hytha and the other servants tell me what they want me to hear. They are devoted to the *viscontesse* and other noble ladies."

"My hope," said the master, "is that Éléonore's opinions will give me a truer picture of the relationships inside the château. And that Perter told her the latest gossip before he finished butchering there."

The alchemist slapped the top edge of the cart's side. "I'm surprised he didn't try to harm your father by attacking you. He must have been tempted while the two of you worked together."

Bertwoin grumbled, "So why give him another chance by having me come to his house?"

"Fear not, Bertwoin. I chose to come while Perter is butchering at a nearby farm. I also don't want him hindering my conversation with his mother-in-law."

Bertwoin sighed. He doubted Alesta would welcome him.

"And while we're on the subject of those who dislike you, plowman, I am told you insulted Sir Philippe's honor so thoroughly that he can no longer ignore your slurs. I will talk with Sir Jean-Luc and have you excused from working there. But I doubt that will keep you safe in the coming months."

Bertwoin glanced at Flowia, who was scowling at him. She had warned him to keep his opinions to himself and, of course, he hadn't obeyed her.

"A boar doesn't act like a sheep," he told her.

"No," Flowia muttered, "it unthinkingly mimics its sire."

"My father is well respected," he argued.

She muttered, "Clanoud is rude and direct/and when

others answer him back/your father calls it disrespect/and so, he always attacks."

Bertwoin couldn't truthfully argue against this, so he stayed quiet. At least he was now learning to rein in his tongue.

Only three geese guarded Éléonore's poultry yard, their number far too paltry to provide a sufficient number of eggs weekly for a family of six. Alesta opened the door, her as face sour as vinegar when she saw Bertwoin, and stood aside without greeting them so they could crowd into the main room.

A crude hearth occupied the room's middle with a tripod straddling its unlit fire pit. The room was chilly, and Bertwoin saw no firewood.

Éléonore moved a stool near the cold hearth for the master. She was a thin woman with smooth skin and the disappointed eyes of a shrew. Her fingers were misshapen, their joints knobby. She looked sideways at them when talking as if she were too ashamed to meet their opinion straightforwardly.

"It's nice of you to bring us something," she whined. "I'm sorry I don't have a fire at the moment to warm you."

The master waved this away. "I'm comfortable. We know the road is bumpy and wearying without a husband, especially while Perter has to work without pay for the château. So we thought a bit of pork would be welcome."

The five of them perked up and stared at the hemp sack with ravenous expressions. Éléonore pointed to her stunted boy. "My man died in the Holy Land right after Raymond here was born. It's only by God's mercy and what Perter brings us and through the charity of people like you that we keep alive."

Embarrassed by their poverty, Bertwoin looked away. The floor was limestone, mostly bare with only a scattering of rushes. Spread out on it near a stool lay a bird net. Someone had been tying it together with considerable skill. The workmanship was precise and pleasing to the eye.

"It's a well-wrought net," he said.

Alesta straightened, her pride as obvious as her nose.

"Well." The master nodded for Flowia to set the hemp sack on a small table. "Don't delay your meal because of us.

Alesta stepped forward before her mother could disagree and opened the sack. She pulled out the joint and ripped off a handful of meat. Instead of chiding Alesta for her lack of manners as Bertwoin's *maman* would have done, Éléonore joined her, pinching off a sliver with her gnarled fingers. She and her daughter tore into the pork like starving vultures, gulping it down and handing meat to the other three children who had rushed forward, mewling, with outstretched hands.

"We'll also bring bread next time," Flowia whispered. The master nodded.

Flowia turned her face away and stared through a square hole that was the room's only window. Bertwoin studied the plank-board shutter held open by a rope tied to a peg hammered into the front wall.

The alchemist watched the feeding frenzy with solemn pity. "I expect food will be less scarce now that Perter has finished his labor days for the *viscontes*."

"We get by," Éléonore said. She scowled at Bertwoin. "As long as no one chases Perter off to the mountains."

"My father's pride made him blind," Bertwoin apologized.

"He's like those in the château," Éléonore said with no forgiveness in her tone. "They all take more than they give."

"I wonder if Mistress Millicent is the same," the alchemist said.

Éléonore took a bite from the hunk of pink pork in her hand. "She's a tough one, don't ever doubt that. Millicent knows well she has a pretty face and uses it to her good. Has all of the men following her like dogs after scraps." With her teeth bared, Éléonore ripped another bite from her greasy handful and said, her words muffled by meat, "Hytha is her good friend."

Alesta gave a bone to her littlest sister, who began to gnaw at the slivers of pork on it.

Éléonore told Alesta, "We'll want the marrow for soup."

Bertwoin wanted to bring Éléonore back to discussing those at the château. "I saw Hytha have a row with Sir Reginald and Sir Philippe."

She snorted. "Sir Reginald. Now there's Devil's meat for you. He'd slit your throat, he would, if you crossed him. Then he'd say he was only adding a second mouth to help you breathe easier. His thoughts about Millicent and Hytha aren't Christian, I can tell you that."

Bertwoin smiled. So Sir Reginald's thoughts were more nightly than knightly. "Do you know anyone in the citadel who would wish to kill Master Servay or Mistress Millicent?"

"The boy wasn't well-liked, but he was no worse than most first-born noble sons. No one in the château, except for Sir Reginald, would have the courage to harm him. As to Mistress Millicent, Sir Reginald claims he carries affection for her, though he gives most of his homage to the *viscontesse*."

"Well, we'll leave you now," said the master.

He rose and grimaced in pain. Both Bertwoin and Flowia stepped forward to help him shuffle outside to the handcart.

As Bertwoin pulled it over the bumpy ground, he said, "They eat like a pack of stray dogs."

"They're half-starved," the master said. "Hunger makes beasts of us all."

"I didn't mean it as an insult. It's just that we treat our hens and ewes better than we do Éléonore and her kind. They have to catch what scraps fall from the tables of others. And it's bad luck to be forced to rely on Perter."

Flowia made a harsh sound in her throat. "He sells some of the meat he earns from butchering for drink, but he does keep them alive. And Éléonore is no more welcome inside the château than the pox. She cannot beg food there even on feast days."

"A sad situation," the master said. "It's left to people like us and the Good Folk to give her what charity we can. The Church, of course, refuses to help an unrepentant heretic."

Mention of the Good Folk and an unrepentant heretic caused Bertwoin to think of Gertrude, Éléonore's sister. She too was familiar with sorrow. She had refused to recant her outlaw beliefs and had stood head up and proud before her accusers, ready to burn for her faith and be remembered as a heretical martyr.

Flowia had taken food to her in the bishop's underground dungeon and later had told Bertwoin that the Church might need to hurry if it wished to use cleansing fire to burn away Gertrude's sins. An uncontrollable chest cough now wracked her thin body. Fever flushed her cheeks. God's death by disease threatened to save her from the Church's death by spectacle and bonfire. Gertrude had thanked Flowia for the food but had refused to accept it; she preferred to slowly starve herself to death.

Pity closed like a fist in Bertwoin's chest. Gertrude had borne the throat-clogging grief of watching her entire family die. The word "orphan" pointed out a motherless child, and the word "widow" marked those who had lost husbands; but what word named a grieving mother who had lost a child or her children?

Éléonore too had lost a child and blamed the seneschal for not saving him.

"Even the abbey refuses them," Bertwoin complained.

"Yes," Flowia said. "Abbot Jehan feeds lepers and beggars but not her. And the château ladies do not forgive their rivals, even after they've been tossed aside." She sighed. "Her family is also shunned because her *grand-mere* was a powerful witch."

Bertwoin had heard of this grandmother. "I'm told she's why the Roman wall on our land still stands. She threw a spell over it so it would never crumble to dust."

"If Éléonore had inherited her witchcraft," Flowia told him, "her chateau enemies would suffer. Her *grand-mere* was one to keep a winter wind under her hat and throw it into the fields of those who displeased her. She caused many hens to lay sour eggs. Few are living now who knew her, but stories of her power are still kept warm."

CHAPTER XXVII.

When Bertwoin came within sight of the master's cottage, he saw his sister, Rachel, waiting for them near the opening in the mulberry hedge. He rushed forward with the master holding onto the cart's sides.

"What's wrong?" Bertwoin asked as he slowed to a stop.

"A boy found some human bones. His mother told the *bayle* our pigs were rooting among them."

"Where?"

"Near the old Roman wall. Papa says the master will want to know this."

"Indeed I do. We must go there at once."

Bertwoin turned the cart aside and hastened toward the Roman ruins with Rachel matching his pace.

"You think they are Master Servay's bones?" Flowia asked.

"If so," the alchemist said, "their current location might be a clue." He sighed. "But they might yet prove to be those of a beggar. Or perhaps they belonged to a sick pilgrim, someone who died before he or she could pray for a cure over Saint Nazarius's shinbone."

"But if they are Master Servay's," Flowia said, "why put them there? That's a long way to haul a corpse."

"There are many who hold a grudge against Clanoud," the master said, his voice quavering as the handcart jolted across a patch of rough ground. "Some would find delight in raining trouble down upon him and his house."

"Even some inside the château," Bertwoin said. "Sir Philippe, for instance."

The alchemist shrugged. "Maybe. But I think we will find that the one who now inconveniences Clanoud is also Master Servay's killer. Sir Philippe probably gave the boy little, if any, attention. And the knight and Sir Jean-Luc seem to be on good terms, though," the master waggled his head, "if there was a hidden quarrel between them, the knight would be our primary suspect. Not only would Master Servay be easy prey for him, but I see a pattern emerging here."

"One with my father and Sir Jean-Luc?" Bertwoin asked.

"Yes, someone's strategy might be to punish the fathers by harming the sons. However, Sir Philippe only fits this pattern if he hated the seneschal."

"So you are saying that putting the corpse on our land accuses me of the boy's murder?"

"Were you not serving at the banquet when Master Servay died?"

"But would I be stupid enough to haul a body to our own land? And let's not forget that Arundel feared Master Servay might cause him to lose his position."

"True, but the defense you just invoked for yourself applies also to the chef. He would never set a murder in his own kitchen. The taint of poison damns the reputation he's so proud of and might end his career."

The alchemist clapped his bony hands. "Anyway, let's hope we are able to determine whether these are Master Servay's desecrated bones. We will look for something telling, a scrap of clothing or some other detail that names the person. The lack of a skull would be one such clue."

He hummed. "A fitting place to find the bones of a headless corpse, don't you think? Roman ruins under the magical spell of a powerful witch."

Rachel glanced at the alchemist in alarm.

He laughed. "Fear not, young woman, unless you intend to disturb its blocks."

She made the sign of the rood.

"Have you not heard the story?" he asked her.

"My father doesn't want a haunted place on our land," Bertwoin explained. "So he doesn't allow anyone to tell us the tale."

"You mean he doesn't want anyone, like Rachel here," Flowia said, "to avoid those woods when he sends them out to gather kindling or mushrooms."

Rachel said to Bertwoin, "Tell me of these stones."

"I only know they have a spell cast over them. But don't worry, Rach, I've touched them plenty of times and never suffered any harm."

The alchemist laughed. "Normally, people would have pilfered all of the stones for building their houses or repairing their kitchens. But the first person, a farmer, who carted away a few of them dropped one on his foot, crushing it while unloading the blocks.

"So he had the cursed stones carted back. Even so, his lameness was a lesson for all to see. Everyone now knew that the spell flung over the wall by Éléonore's grandmother still protected it even after Death's scythe had cut her down.

"To add further weight to this lesson, another farmer later stole a few blocks and died soon afterward of a fever. No one wishes to become the third example."

"So we're safe as long as we don't steal the stones," Bertwoin told his sister.

Though called a Roman wall, all that was left of it was an unsteady corner of limestone blocks, furred by lichen and moss. When they came to the ruins, they found two of the *bayle's* men sitting nearby with their backs against a maple. One had an unstrung bow lying on the grass beside him, the other an oak staff. Bones lay piled in front of them.

The young man with a bow nodded to Flowia, who nodded back.

Bertwoin helped the master climb out of the handcart and painfully creep to the jumbled skeleton. Two pigs came grunting out of the woods to see if their friend, Bertwoin, had brought them more meat.

"They're human," the master said. "Let's lay them out to see how tall the person was." He glanced around. "Then we'll search for scraps of cloth or anything else we can find."

The middle-aged man with an oak staff said, "The *bayle* told us to guard these bones and said nothing about letting anyone mess with them."

The master dismissed this obstacle with the flick of a hand. "The *bayle* will have no objection to my examining them. We intend to make his job easier."

The guard shook his head. "He didn't say anything to us about your coming."

"Maybe you should go ask him," Flowia said.

"That's a long way to walk, and who knows where he is."

"Let them examine the bones," the bowman said.

"You don't give orders here."

"It's on your head then." The young man got up and glanced at the crumbling wall. "I don't like being here anyway." He nodded again to Flowia and faded into the woods with his bow.

Flowia whispered to Bertwoin, "I tended his mother when she came down with the flux."

Bertwoin walked over to the sitting man and stepped on

the staff lying beside him so he couldn't pick it up. The *bayle's* man shrugged. "Well, don't carry any of them off."

Though some bones were missing, Bertwoin and Flowia and Rachel pieced together a skeleton while the alchemist, the guard, and two curious pigs watched them. Then when they scoured the area, Flowia found a fleshed finger the pigs had left at the base of a pink rock rose. They didn't find a skull.

The master clapped his hands. "I think we're done here." With Bertwoin's help, he climbed back onto his small chariot and settled before his human ox pulled him away. Rachel left them to return home.

"The bones are of Master Servay's stature," Flowia said once they were beyond the guard's hearing.

The master hummed agreement. "And the skull is missing. The bones are thick enough to suggest a male, and the finger shows little evidence of manual labor. We must also consider the timing. Young Servay disappears, and a skeleton is found just long enough afterward to have given a herd of hungry hogs time to strip the flesh from the bones. So it would be a considerable coincidence if these were *not* his remains."

Flowia sighed. "So are you going to tell Sir Jean-Luc and the *visconte* that Master Servay's body was fed to pigs like offal?"

"I think, daughter," the master said, his tone slow and musing, "that we should let the *bayle* decide what to tell the father about his son's skeleton. We need only tell the lawman that, indeed, we believe these are Master Servay's bones."

Bertwoin cleared his throat. "Do you think the *bayle* will come to arrest my father? Or me?"

"He does like the simplest answer," the alchemist said. "He has one body lost and one skeleton found. And the bones *were* found on *your* land." Annoyed, the master again slapped the top of the handcart's wooden side.

CHAPTER XXVIII.

The following day, Bertwoin was sitting in his kitchen eating breakfast porridge when Wilfraed breezed into the house and announced, "Flowia is here again."

Uncle Laurence huffed and rose from the bench along one side of the table. "This has got to stop," he said and stalked toward the front door.

"Wait," Bertwoin yelled.

But his uncle ignored him and slammed the door behind him.

When Bertwoin stood up, Clanoud told him, "Let him have his say with her."

"He hates her more than the taxman. He might hit her."

His *maman* shook her head. "She'll argue him down."

"If he hits her, she'll go at him with her knife."

"For slapping her?" his father said in disbelief. "Who does she think she is?"

"Do you let anybody slap you?" Bertwoin challenged.

"That's not-"

Uncle Laurence jerked open the front door and stomped back inside, leaving it open. "You need to go out to her. *Now*."

After a moment of surprise, Bertwoin rushed past him. When he saw Flowia's triumphant smile, he let out his breath.

He went to her, aching to take her in his arms and kiss her, but his sister Rachel stood off to one side and watched them with greedy curiosity. Flowia's smile softened; she knew of his desire to touch her.

His *maman* appeared in the doorway. She nodded to Flowia, who returned the silent greeting.

"We need to go now," Flowia told him.

"Gladly." He grinned at her, but when she didn't return his smile, doubt fluttered in his stomach.

"Is the master well?"

"Sir Philippe has accused you publicly of murdering Master Servay and of trying to kill Mistress Millicent."

"Me?"

"Sir Jean-Luc has already sent a boy to Tisbe's to fetch the *bayle*. The master says for you to flee to our house. He will accompany you to the château." She raised her hand to stop him from interrupting her. "But he's still lame as a poacher's excuse. So you'll have to pull him all the way to the citadel in our handcart so he can defend you."

"To the château? Why would I go there? I need to hide somewhere until the master solves these crimes. If I appear before the seneschal and the master doesn't convince him I'm innocent, I'll be tortured and hung."

"He thinks it best if you launch a surprise attack against this accusation. An innocent man who doesn't fear justice would do so."

"But Sir Philippe is a nobleman. I'm just a peasant. And why should we even pretend this charge is true?"

"God will be on your side. And the master will be your advocate."

"The Devil often gets His way too," Bertwoin reminded her.

"Do you think I don't know that?" she muttered.

THE GUARD SLOUCHED AT THE CHÂTEAU'S EAST GATE peered out from under his square helmet with disbelief and dropped his hand to the hilt of his sheathed sword. Bertwoin tried to look relaxed and innocent as he pulled the handcart up to the sentry, who hopped like an alert crow in front of them. When the guard's eyes darted to the alchemist sitting behind Bertwoin, his expression turned wary.

Bertwoin felt a solid weight of doubt lift like a yoke off of his neck. Maybe seizing the initiative and boldly challenge this spiteful accusation had been the best choice. If their coming startled and flustered a sentry, might it not also confound Sir Philippe?

The guard's aggressive behavior, of course, aroused the curiosity and tongues of the people flowing in and out of the château. Spying a soldier among the throng of incoming foot traffic, the sentry ordered him to find the captain of the guards and tell him the plowman was at the gate.

They didn't have to wait long. Almost immediately a captain of the guards, straight-backed and grim as a winter storm, strutted out to them.

"Come," he said, his manner brusque and official. "I have already sent word to the seneschal. He's with the *visconte* in the Great Hall."

He led them into the crowded forecourt where a butcher Bertwoin didn't know worked under the elms.

Bertwoin pulled the handcart as near as possible to the keep, where the Great Hall occupied an upper floor. Despite himself, his hands were clammy. The Great Hall was where young *Visconte* Raimon-Rogièr held important gatherings, celebrations, and feasts; but it was also where he sat in judgment of criminals. And they hadn't come to celebrate a saint's day or to attend a banquet.

The captain pulled open a seldom-used door where a stairway led to the back entrance of the Great Hall. Bertwoin heard the noise of Arundel's kitchen, which had direct access through an open door to these back stairs.

The captain lunged up two flights of stairs to a narrow landing where he waited while Bertwoin helped the master hobble up the slippery stone steps. Making the alchemist's ascent even more difficult was the fact that the height of the steps varied and some were uneven so enemies might stumble as they fought their way upward. Bertwoin wasn't their enemy, of course, but those living in the Château Comtal might now consider him one.

After knocking and waiting for some time, they were allowed to enter a majestic room which would not have been out of place in a grand cathedral. The small door they came through was set in the middle of the Great Hall's side wall. To their right, a raised platform ran across the back wall. On it, *Visconte* Raimon-Rogièr sat enthroned in a high-backed chair. Behind him hung his red-and-white coat-of-arms with its black fingerling fish. Above it, light glared in through a high window.

Sir Jean-Luc stood beside the *visconte*, wary as a loyal mastiff. Bertwoin swallowed. He saw no gratitude in the seneschal's fierce stare for his having saved the man's daughter. Did he really believe Sir Philippe's spiteful accusation?

Bertwoin helped the alchemist hobble toward the dais,

passing windows set in the wall on their left that were tall enough for a man to stand in. Tapestries—mostly hunting scenes—hung between these windows.

Young *Visconte* Raimon-Rogièr studied him a moment without expression. Then he turned his gaze on the limping alchemist, and his face softened with concern.

"Are you well, master?"

"I am in the throes of a laming disease, Lord Raimond-Rogièr. It feels as if I walk on broken bones, but it will pass."

The *visconte* signaled for a servant to bring a chair and set it on the platform beside him. This honoring of the master partially restored Bertwoin's hopes. Maybe the wily alchemist could offset Sir Jean-Luc's obvious hostility.

The master shuffled up the two steps onto the platform and seated himself beside his lord with a sigh of relief. All three men now faced Bertwoin, who stood alone below them.

The *visconte's* expression was neutral, Sir Jean-Luc's angry, and the master alchemist, *Deo Gratias*, looked encouraging as well as benign.

A single knock resounded through the grand room. At a nod from Sir Jean-Luc, a soldier opened one of the high double doors at the other end of the Great Hall. Sir Philippe sauntered inside, coming from a shadowy landing into a slash of light thrown across the room by the high window behind the platform. Gidie marched in behind Sir Philippe followed by the *bayle*, who looked as if he had missed his usual ale and breakfast at Tisbe's tavern.

Sir Philippe saw the master sitting beside the *visconte*, and his eyes narrowed. He greeted his lord with a bow, then examined Bertwoin with the pleased look of a poacher seeing a rabbit caught in one of his traps. Bertwoin turned back to face the trio of judges on the dais and tried to look confident.

Visconte Raimon-Rogièr also examined the rabbit a

moment before he told him, "This is not yet a court or official proceeding. First, I wish to hear from you and your accuser," he gestured at Sir Philippe, "before I determine whether I need to act upon these heinous charges brought against you."

Bertwoin bowed, "I thank you, my lord." He sucked in his bottom lip and didn't add that he was sorry this false charge was wasting everyone's time.

The *visconte* nodded to Sir Jean-Luc, who snapped out, "We have a witness who saw you pour poison into my daughter's mead when you served Sir Reginald at the feast."

Though his heart drummed behind his breast bone, Bertwoin willed himself to appear calm. He glanced at Sir Philippe's squire, probably his accuser and maybe also the witness. Gidie was the loose knot in the room, the one he needed to untie.

"This witness lied," he told the seneschal.

"And why would he have done so?"

"I can only know that if I know who accused me."

"The fact that you are singled out and accused at all seems to indicate a want of innocence," Sir Jean-Luc said. He waved for Gidie to step forward.

"This report was brought to you?" Sir Jean-Luc asked the squire.

Gidie nodded deferentially. "Yes, sir. A man of character told me he saw this plowman pour poison from a glass vial into your daughter's mead."

So the squire was not the witness. He had another enemy, a hidden one. He didn't expect them to tell him who had accused him of this attempted murder. They didn't want to give him or his formidable father the opportunity to persuade the witness to disavow the accusation.

Sir Jean-Luc stroked his beard a moment, then glanced with suspicion at the alchemist, who stiffened.

Bertwoin realized the master had not come just to defend him but also to protect himself and Flowia. If it were true that he, Bertwoin, had attempted to murder Mistress Millicent, then where did he get his poison if not from the alchemist or his virgin? The words "glass vial" pointed blame at the master, who used them in his work. Few people owned them.

Turning back to the squire, the seneschal stood with his arms across his chest. "Why bring this to you, not the *bayle* or me?"

Gidie pointed at Bertwoin. "This arrogant peasant insulted my knight by despoiling his meat and drink, though not with poison. The man felt it was his duty to bring what he saw to your ear but thought it best to do so by going through my knight, who has also been aggrieved by this plowman's crimes. The witness wishes not to be named." He waved at Bertwoin. "This peasant's family is known for its violence."

"And you believe that if he tried to murder my daughter, he is also the one who killed my son?"

"Such a conclusion comes natural, sir."

The seneschal nodded, then snarled at Bertwoin, "You still deny this charge?"

"I do, sir."

"And why do you think this witness selected you?"

"Perhaps," the alchemist said, "it was maliciously done."

"And you think that those who brought the charge to me lack the ability to judge the accuser's character?"

Bertwoin said, "Those who pass along these false charges do so because it serves their purposes. They bear false witness, and in so doing, hinder us from finding your son's true killer."

The master shook his head slightly, his eyes half-closed in displeasure. A more conciliatory tone was wanted.

"Ah," the seneschal said, "so you are saying the squire has a grudge against you?"

"He does."

"Pray tell me, why would that be?"

"I unhorsed both of Sir Philippe's squires when they attacked me at my home."

Sir Jean-Luc looked with disbelief at Gidie. "This is true?"

His face reddening, the squire said, "We were unarmed."

"And he was armed?"

"He carried a long hoe."

Visconte Raimon-Rogièr brayed laughter. "A hoe? Two squires unhorsed by a hoe?" He waved at Bertwoin. "Let's make this plowman a knight. Minstrels will soon sing of his deeds."

"Why would this plowman have a reason to kill my son?" Sir Jean-Luc asked the squire, bringing a sober tone back into their meeting.

Gidie shrugged. "I know not the reason, sir."

Sir Philippe suggested, "Perhaps the plowman can be persuaded to tell us that."

"It is premature for the use of torture," the alchemist said. "The *visconte* has not yet decided whether to proceed with this charge, *and* it is not your prerogative to make that judgment, knight."

"Nor yours, goldsmith."

The alchemist frowned. "And the bellows boy is problematic."

"The bellows boy?" Sir Philippe asked, his tone derisive.

"Yes, he drank from Master Servay's bitter cup and died of the same poison that killed the seneschal's son and almost killed his daughter. Mistress Millicent is alive now because of the quick action taken by this plowman you now accuse. A plowman, I might add, who was not present inside Château Comtal when the bellows boy was killed."

Sir Philippe, acting bored by the alchemist's arguments, said, "He might have used a confederate inside the kitchen. I believe one of the cooks wishes to marry this peasant's sister. I pity the man."

The master looked at Bertwoin for confirmation and received a nod. "So," the alchemist said, "if he did use a confederate, then the plowman here isn't the one you are accusing of murdering Master Servay. And you have no proof against him. Your charge seems more an act of revenge for the unhorsing of your squires than one of reporting the true killer."

"We have a witness," Gidie said.

"And how reliable is this witness? You yourself said that the person who attempted to kill Sir Jean-Luc's daughter is the same person who killed his son. And I agree. Murderers normally use the same pattern for all their crimes once the method has proven successful."

"Well, master, you know murderers better than I do," Sir Philippe said with lazy sarcasm. "And speaking of better," he drawled, "you and this peasant accuse my squire and me of passing on lies. This plowman mocks us at every turn. He believes he is equal or even better than we."

Everyone stared at Bertwoin. "That is not true, sir," he said. "I acknowledge that those who fight protect us and keep all of us safe, nobles and churchmen and peasants alike. That is, those who *actuaUy* fight."

Sir Philippe took a threatening step toward Bertwoin, who didn't flinch away. "The peasant dares to mock me publicly before my lord."

The alchemist glared at Bertwoin. To divert the conversation, Bertwoin said, "I did not serve Mistress Millicent. I didn't touch the food or drink of anyone who sat at the high table except for Sir Reginald's. He and the chamberlain are my witnesses for this."

Sir Philippe sniffed. "It would be easy in the confusion and bustle for you to quickly pour poison into the mead while everyone else was too busy to notice. But someone did notice. Someone saw you do this."

"That someone lies. I never approached the sideboard or entered the larder where the mead waited to be served." When the knight scorned his denial with a contemptuous expression, Bertwoin added, "And as to this confusion you speak of, sir, the *visconte's* feasts are not melees. The chamberlain doesn't allow a plowman to simply take what he wills from the sideboard."

The *visconte* smiled, momentarily amused by his boldness.

Sir Philippe glared at him. "I did not imply that the château feasts were chaotic, yokel."

"I am sorry, sir. Your use of the word 'confusion,' confused me."

"This is a serious issue, peasant," Sir Jean-Luc shouted, startling everyone. He jabbed a finger at Bertwoin's face. "You will cease mocking this proceeding by insulting one of our knights."

After a moment of profound silence, Sir Philippe raised a fist. "And I'll not bandy words with a peasant. He ridicules me in public. The accusation has weight, and I stand behind it. I demand justice for Master Servay."

"As do I," said Sir Jean-Luc, his words resounding across the cavernous room. "If I may be so bold as to suggest a solution to this problem, your Grace, I ask that the master alchemist and this plowman be given three days, until Sunday mass, to find the murderer. If they cannot, then the plowman should be persuasively questioned on this matter. He might not be so flippant then."

Bertwoin felt like a worm ripped from the earth and left shriveling on a hot rock in the sun.

"What prevents him from fleeing?" Sir Philippe asked.

Bertwoin said, "I will not flee, though we are given this impossible task."

"Oh," Sir Philippe said with contempt, "we now have the inviolable word of a peasant."

"The word," Bertwoin answered, "of a plowman whose father *fought* in the Holy Land."

"It is still only a peasant's promise," Sir Philippe drawled. "And you are not your father. You are also not a nobleman, though you think yourself as good as one."

"True, it is only the word of a peasant," the alchemist said. "Unlike a nobleman's promise, his pledge doesn't require a hostage to ensure he doesn't lie." He paused to let everyone consider his comment, then added, "You have no proof for this charge, sir. And you provide no witness for us to question. This plowman's main crimes seem to be his belief that you are a coward and his ability to defeat squires with a hoe."

The *visconte* glanced at his seneschal, who said, "Don't mock us, alchemist. Who are you to disapprove of the laws we knights live by? Paying scutage is not an act of cowardice."

"And don't you mock me, seneschal, with this ridiculous charge. I *am* trying to find your son's killer."

"Then do it." Sir Jean-Luc turned to Sir Philippe. "The plowman won't flee, because if he does, his family shall forfeit their house and all of their goods."

It was a punishment worse than death for any family. They would starve to death as outcasts. Just the shame of it would kill his proud father.

Young *Visconte* Raimon-Rogièr raised a hand to halt the bickering. He turned to the alchemist. "You purport to show me who *didn't* kill my cousin." He waved toward Bertwoin. "Like Sir Jean-Luc, I wish to know who *did*. Bring me the name in three days or bring me back this plowman."

"That will be difficult to prove, my lord."

"Three days, master goldsmith."

"You burden me with an impossible task, my lord."

"On the contrary, master goldsmith, I show great faith in you. I think if pressed, you and this witty plowman will solve this puzzle for us. And I give Clanoud's son three day's grace because I am grateful that he saved Mistress Millicent. You have my decision. These proceedings are now concluded."

CHAPTER XXIX.

The alchemist's expression was stern and he stayed quiet as Bertwoin pulled him through the château's East Gate, then along the citadel's winding streets, and through the outer wall's Narbonne Gate. Bertwoin mentally chided himself for disappointing the master. The *visconte* thought his answers entertaining, but his unruly tongue made others his enemies.

The alchemist stayed silent the entire way home. When they reached the poultry yard and the geese announced their arrival, the master startled as if coming awake. Bertwoin realized the alchemist had been wandering the wilderness of his thoughts. He wasn't angry with him after all…or not overly so.

Roland came grunting out to greet them and shoved his bulk against Bertwoin's leg to claim the back scratch he thought everyone owed him. When they entered the cottage, he accompanied them and trotted over to his goddess, who stooped to scribble her fingernails in the unreachable spot behind his ear.

Meat hanging from ceiling beams and decaying rushes on the floor gave the room a sweet smell. Bertwoin took a deep breath and savored the homey smell. Things he rarely noticed now seemed important and delightful.

His expression grim, the alchemist pointed Bertwoin to the bench along one side of the kitchen table and sat in a chair on the other side. Flowia left Roland as a piggy puddle of jubilant flesh on the floor and poured ale for them.

The master rapped the table with his knuckles and told Flowia, "We have three days to find the murderer or Bertwoin is forfeit."

"Oh, no." She clasped a hand over her mouth.

Bertwoin told her of Sir Philippe's accusation, of Sir Jean-Luc's lack of gratitude for his saving Mistress Millicent, of the *visconte's* decision, and that this time he didn't have the options of fleeing or hiding.

"We must not allow fear to muddle our thinking," the alchemist said. "Let us start with what we know and ask simple yet discerning questions. Master Servay was almost poisoned by tainted cider and later died after eating larks. Why this drink and why this food?"

"The simple answer," Flowia said, "is that they were the drink and food specially prepared for the seneschal's son."

"Yes, so the poisoner is someone with access to the kitchen and someone who knows the eating habits of the *visconte* and his guests. As for Mistress Millicent, she wasn't the only one who drank mead, but her dishes and goblet were marked out with her sign. So it must be someone who works in the kitchen or visits it so often they are barely noticed. This someone also has ready access to poisons and is an expert in using them. Dosing the cider and mead was easy enough. But how does one poison a lark without anyone noticing? The bird's breast was sewn together over the stuffing. Could the poisoner have poured the belladonna between the stitches?"

Bertwoin snapped his fingers. "That's where I saw the

knot. There were two stuffed birds on a table in the kitchen, and their feet were tied together with different knots. One had a fancy knot, tied like those I saw on the bird net in Éléonore's house."

"Éléonore knows well the properties of plants," Flowia said. "But she is forbidden to visit Château Comtal."

Bertwoin said, "But Perter was in and out of the kitchen every day he butchered meat for them. So our murderer is *two* people working as one."

"Which I fear is the argument they will throw back at us," the master said, "if we don't prove that Bertwoin is innocent." He looked pointedly at Flowia. "He doesn't have the requisite knowledge of poisons."

"But I do," she said.

"Yes, daughter, you do."

"We have seen how those in power will blame murders on others," she said. "They may dismiss our evidence by saying that other women tie their nets with these same knots. And most women know the ways of poisonous plants. In small doses, we all use them as medicine. They may decide not to accuse me and accuse his mother instead."

Bertwoin shook his fists. "Oh, if only I knew who witnesses against me."

"Yes," the alchemist said, "it must be someone who was able to speak with the squire. Not Éléonore, then. Perter himself? Or was there a third conspirator?"

"Are we certain," Bertwoin asked, "it was the pig-sticker who killed Master Servay, and if so, how do we prove it?"

"I have little doubt," the master said, "that Éléonore and Perter are responsible for these murders. Our main problem is convincing Sir Philippe. He wants Bertwoin punished. And he seems to wield influence with the seneschal. So we will have to bring our Doubting Thomases incontestable proof of Éléonore and Perter's guilt."

"How is that possible?" Bertwoin asked.

"What say you to a confession in front of witnesses?"

"They're not fools."

"We are all fools in our own way," the master said. "Because of his pride, Perter is the easier target of the two. He wants to be thought of as shrewd, and he drinks in the same tavern where the head was found." The old man looked pointedly at Bertwoin. "Sometimes those who wish to be called clever say things that harm them."

Bertwoin sighed. "My father has beaten me often for this fault, and Flowia chastises me for it. Yet I have been too headstrong to accept their guidance. So now, when I look to blame someone for my plight, I point a finger at my own chest."

"Well," the master said. "Accepting responsibility is the first step toward change. And now we must make Perter's words betray him. To do this, we will goad his vanity. Flowia, go tell the *bayle* to come to me. We wish to help him catch Master Servay's killer."

Bertwoin laughed. "It's odd, isn't it? Our using a bird net to catch a burly pig-butcher."

Flowia clapped her hands. "And what is a net but five hundred holes tied together by strands of thick thread."

The alchemist smiled at her. "Let's hope the butcher only sees the spaces and not what binds them until it is too late and he is entangled."

CHAPTER XXX.

A gain Bertwoin lurked in ambush behind a thorn-ridden gorse, its almond-shaped blooms glowing like a ghostly swarm of yellow butterflies in the wan moonlight. Nervous butterflies also seemed to flutter in his stomach. The empty, dreaming Roman road stretched into the mysterious dark. Tonight, he heard no music from Tisbe's tavern, only drunken laughter interrupted from time to time by gleeful shouts. He kept the woolen hood on his cloak pulled over his head and endured the tireless breeze.

Instead of wielding a wheel spoke, Bertwoin had come armed tonight with a staff made of strong ash. This time, he intended to face the pig-butcher. Of course, he also carried his knife, but he expected his staff to be enough protection. And he didn't feel guilty or think he had any need to confess a sin. What he was about to do was condoned by others.

No Roman elephant ghosted by, though he watched for it. He remembered the alchemist telling him, "Yes, the vestiges of Rome's indomitable power still haunt us to this day." The master had winked and added, "But people's tales of those times are disjoined from the truth. Even the beast's name is lost to us. It was the consul who was called Domitius, not the elephant."

Chuckling at Bertwoin's disappointment, the old man had waggled his head. "Who can blame our ancestors for seeing this fearsome creature stomping about and finding it much more awe-inspiring than a mere man? So they remembered only the mighty beast and mixed up its name with that of its owner."

Bertwoin shrugged. "Does the name really matter?"

The master raised a bony finger. "It provides us with two truths. First, that others who are more powerful than we are pin their names to our good works, and then we are forgotten. Second, that true power lies not with the beast but with the one who controls it."

A movement just beyond the moonlit edge of the road caught Bertwoin's eye. He rose into a squat and peered in the direction of Tisbe's tavern until two shapes walked out of the dark and solidified into a man and a woman. Bertwoin breathed deeply to settle his nerves, stood up, and grabbed his staff. Like a robber ready to demand money and possessions, he strolled out to the rutted road's grassy middle, keeping his cloak's hood up over his head.

Perter stuttered a step, but he didn't stop. Despite his deep-seated loathing for the pig-sticker, Bertwoin had to admire the man's courage.

Bertwoin watched Perter slouch toward him and draw his dagger. Wary as an alert stag, the pig-bleeder scanned their surroundings to make sure they were alone. Alesta had stopped seven or eight paces behind him.

Bertwoin waited until he could see Perter's distrustful but resolute expression before he said, "I have come to warn you, pig-man. My father is hunting for you. Maybe you should return to tending sheep in the mountains."

"And you do this favor for me because we are such good friends?"

"I do it for Éléonore's sake. She and her family will need what you can send them from the mountains."

"Your lie is out of tune, plowman. If you can't lie better than that, you had better always tell the truth." He chuckled. "So why is testy Clanoud grumbling about me now?"

"Because you threw Master Servay's corpse on our land. He calls you out as a murderer."

Perter grunted and again scanned their moonlit surroundings. "Me? I murder pigs, fart-sniffer, not people. It's what I do for my work."

Bertwoin pointed one end of his staff at the butcher. "My father says you killed a bellows boy, though that was more by accident than by plan. He says you're the coward who poisoned Master Servay and Mistress Millicent."

Alesta faded into the darkness, fleeing back toward Tisbe's tavern. There would be no angel story this time.

"Coward, am I?" Taking another step closer, Perter sneered, "Why do *you* wait for me here, furrow-hopper? Did you know that this was the very spot where an angel flew down from heaven and blessed me with its touch?"

"What I know is that you moved freely about in the château," Bertwoin said. "I know you brought a lark of your own into the kitchen and probably took one home with you. I know it was you who poured the juice of death cherries into Mistress Millicent's mead. I know it was you who stole Master Servay's body from the chapel."

Perter growled laughter. "*Viscontesse* Agnes says an angel came down and wafted the body away to heaven. Who are you to gainsay her?"

"One who knows it was a black-hearted rascal who stole the corpse and cut off its head."

Perter again scanned the gorse bushes before he asked, "Is

this what peasant heroes do? They make up fairy tales and jump out from behind bushes and scare people in the dark? Tell me, mule's-ass, why is this knight's brat so important to you? Why have you come here for him?"

"Because," Bertwoin blurted out, "I'm the one they're accusing of killing Master Servay."

Perter raised his arms in triumph toward the night sky spattered with stars. "So, the puffed-up hero is now a lowly murderer." He flicked his hand, shooing Bertwoin away. "Run off to the mountains, boy, before the *bayle* catches you. I'll let everyone know Clanoud's son has become a shepherd. But before you go, tell me how you stole the whelp's body out from under the priest's nose."

"You tell me, butcher."

"Me? I figured a demon had crept into the chapel and spirited away the brat's corpse. The same demon, of course, killed the walking pustule."

Bertwoin readied his staff. "Let's go find the *bayle*, pigsticker, and hear what he thinks of your demon story."

Something slammed into the back of Bertwoin's skull. Stars burst in front of his eyes. He shook his head, blinking, and realized he had fallen forward onto his knees.

Perter picked up his staff. Alesta walked around Bertwoin and stood beside her husband.

"Good girl," the pig-man said.

So she hadn't fled after all. Bertwoin moaned. He had to keep the butcher talking. "You were only Éléonore's lackey, weren't you? It's the women of your household who are the clever ones. They planned out this revenge, then trained you to do tricks for them."

"You think Éléonore remembered the chapel's windows?" the pig-killer blurted out.

Bertwoin looked up at the pig-butcher's smile. Had the man just confessed?

"But it was she who gave you the potion for drugging the religieux's ale."

Perter shrugged. "Is that what the magic man says?" His derision was as sharp as a honed blade. "That while the drugged priest slept, I crept into the chapel like a little mouse." He hunched his shoulders forward and moved his hands like shuffling mice feet. "Did he say I shoved the whelp's body out of a window, then ran down to haul it away in my waiting cart?"

"Let's go," Alesta whined.

Bertwoin frowned. Did people know that the murderer had used a window? After the master told the *visconte* how the killer had stolen the body, had the news scattered across the domain like thistledown in the wind?

Grinning, Perter tapped the side of Bertwoin's head with the staff. "And what did I do with the snotty pup's body, furrow-hopper? Bury it? Or did I cart it to the wall on your land? Clanoud ought to thank me for feeding his pigs."

"Hah, you only did it to throw blame on me."

"You're talking too much," Alesta told her husband.

"Shut your mouth."

Perter leaned toward Bertwoin as if to whisper a secret. "But that wouldn't be revenge enough, would it? Not for a churlish peasant like me. No, if it was me, I would butcher out brat's organ meats and sneak them back into the château so Sir Jean-Luc and the other Château Comtal prigs might dine on one of their own. They do enjoy their stews and sausages."

Bertwoin stared at him, speechless with shock.

The butcher jittered with glee. "Ah, you're stunned. You think me a fiend loosed from Hell." His smile faded away. "But is it not Éléonore's right to claim revenge for wrongs done to her? 'An eye for an eye, a tooth for a tooth,' the Good

Book tells us. Nothing says this law holds true only for nobles."

As Bertwoin realized the depths of the butcher's depravity, he thanked God for the alchemist's simple but cunning plan. He told himself to stay quiet, advice he rarely heeded, and to not disturb the flood of Perter's bragging.

His moonlit expression radiant with proud contempt, the pig-sticker explained, "Sir Jean-Luc threw Éléonore aside as if she were a scrap of meat for his mastiff. And those in the château gloated while Éléonore watched her precious boy die. Instead of helping to save him, Sir Jean-Luc and the château she-wolves laughed at her suffering. So why shouldn't the seneschal also suffer the loss of his children?"

"What are you going to do with me?" Bertwoin asked.

"Nothing. Well, maybe bash you about a bit." Perter wiggled the staff in front of Bertwoin's eyes.

"You've told him everything," Alesta complained.

"Told him what? I never said a thing. He made it all up to save his own neck." He sighed with pleasure. "It'll be fun to watch him hang and know that he knows what happened. Clanoud will be brought low. I will have my revenge."

"He's dangerous alive," she argued.

"He'll hang. I set Sir Philippe on him, which was as easy as aiming a terrier at a rat."

The *bayle* rose behind the row of gorse bushes and swaggered out onto the road with a sergeant following him. Perter faced them. Alesta darted into a dark field.

Perter glanced back at Bertwoin and said with savage contempt, "You're a traitor to your own kind."

"I've heard enough," the *bayle* said, rounding the bushes. "You'll come with us, pig-butcher, and we'll let you tell your evil tale to the seneschal. I don't think he'll find it entertaining, but I guarantee you that after he hears your story, you'll scream in agony for days before you're hanged, disembow-eled, then drawn and quartered."

As the sergeant strode toward him, the pig-sticker glanced off to one side, startled. Everyone glanced in the same direction. Perter shoved the sergeant off balance, turned, and fled around Bertwoin, who flung himself sideways and grabbed at the butcher's ankle. His grip wasn't strong enough to hold the foot, but it tripped Perter, who fell and slid half an arm's length on the dirt road.

Perter scrambled onto his hands and knees, but the *bayle* and his man reached him before he had risen to his feet. The sergeant clubbed the side of his skull, knocking him groaning to the ground.

Bertwoin thought it odd that the butcher kept getting bashed in this place. It was as if fate enjoyed playing a prank on him.

"He'll claim he never confessed," Bertwoin told the *bayle*, "but I think he said enough."

"He did."

Bertwoin nodded his thanks and began marching toward the alchemist's cottage where the master and Flowia waited to hear whether their plan had succeeded.

Had Alesta already reached home and warned Éléonore? Would they now slip away? An empty feeling in Bertwoin's stomach marked his doubts. They would never escape. Her relatives were more likely to turn her over to the authorities than to hide her.

CHAPTER XXXI

Not quite sure how he felt, Bertwoin trotted all the way to the alchemist's cottage. Yes, the threat of his torture and death had vanished, and his family was now safe again; but he had helped destroy Éléonore and her household.

His abrupt intrusion into the master's poultry yard startled the dozing geese into a clamor. Roland grunted a challenge and stood his ground, ready to defend his home and its feathered flock. Bertwoin complimented the boar with a polite huff. Roland returned the greeting and accepted a friendly back scratch, which lasted only two breaths because Flowia jerked open the front door and peered outside, her figure haloed by faint candlelight behind her.

She rushed out to him. He pulled her aside where the master couldn't see them and joyfully kissed her. Panting a little, they entered the cottage.

The master examined his face and relaxed with a shoulder-dropping sigh. "So our subterfuge worked."

Flowia danced over to a clay jug and served them tankards of new red wine, milky-white goat's cheese, and slices of pear.

Bertwoin's retelling of his face-off with the pig-butcher took on an even more somber tone when he told of Perter's brag that Arundel had served morsels of Master Servay's flesh to the seneschal and others at Château Comtal.

The master stared across the candlelit kitchen into the shadowy front room. "I once heard the story of a man who angered the Greek pagan gods by doing the same thing. The depth of Perter's hatred surprises me. Was the child who died his son? Doubtful, yet he might still have loved Éléonore's boy. Excessive love might have provoked his willingness to claim this insane revenge."

The alchemist shook his head in disgust. "Here I am, an old fool, thrusting love without any proof into the breast of a butcher. Why do I strive to ennoble Perter's despicable motives? They cannot be justified."

" The old man stretched, then said, "You did well, Bertwoin. I'm off to rest my tired bones. I'll talk with the *bayle* tomorrow morning and find out whether Sir Jean-Luc accepted Perter's guilt. Sleep well, you two, and dream well."

Flowia walked Bertwoin partway home. Roland escorted them, grunting from time to time to let them know where he was, especially when he was off exploring something interesting in the night woods. He assumed his presence was important to them. So he was especially crestfallen when they made a nest in the silky grass and kept shoving him away.

Bertwoin returned to the alchemist's house the following afternoon. The master sat as usual on a sturdy oak stool beside his oven, though today no fire burned in its iron belly. Flowia sat on a bench with two buckets at her feet, washing pottery and beakers and other glassware. She smiled a welcome to him, then stared down at the buckets, her lips compressed, her expression tight.

Bertwoin's elation turned to worry. He stared at her a moment, but she didn't lift her eyes to him. What had gone amiss?

Bertwoin asked, "Did it not go well with the *bayle* today, master?"

"Yes. With Perter, matters went as expected. His bragging condemns him."

Bertwoin let out a long breath. "And how is your toe, master?"

"Ah well, I have little discomfort now. So the trek to the château this morning was not painful. And you, plowman? Do you rejoice in having proved that Sir Philippe's accusation against you was baseless?"

"I do. And I will avoid him like the night does the day. He will seek revenge. But it was you who solved the murders, not me. My family now raises their bowls and drink to you whenever your name is mentioned."

The alchemist ducked his head to acknowledge the honor they did him. Then making certain Bertwoin watched him, he poured a clear, thick liquid into a tall, flat-bottomed glass tube and said, "I wish Sir Jean-Luc were as grateful."

"He should be," Flowia said. "We prevented the death of his only daughter." She raised her chin to catch Bertwoin's attention, pointed to a linen cloth, then nodded toward a table where wet glassware glinted with reflected candlelight. "You can dry these."

The alchemist chuckled, but his amusement vanished quickly, and his mood again turned solemn. There was silence then as Flowia washed a cucurbit in a bucket of soapy water, rinsed it in the second bucket, and set it on the table for Bertwoin to dry.

The alchemist dropped two orange lumps into the clear

liquid and watched them sink like fisherman's bait to the glass tube's wide bottom.

Bertwoin said, "I don't think Alesta ever told Perter that I was the one who ambushed him. Why favor me so and keep this from him?"

Flowia raised her eyebrows. "I thought we agreed when Na Thea was here that this saved her husband from ridicule, and at the same time made him special. Also by keeping quiet, Alesta prevented a feud from rising between their family and yours." Flowia touched her chest over her heart to show respect. "She had the cunning of a fox."

"Well, she did me a grand favor, and I'll do what I can for her and even her mother. What Éléonore did was a wicked crime, but Sir Jean-Luc did treat her with contempt and did ruin her life. She and her family suffered. Let God judge and punish her, not us."

"Ah well," the master said. "She has already escaped our judgment."

The old goldsmith's funereal tone warned Bertwoin that all had not gone well with Éléonore. He looked at Flowia for an explanation.

She stared down at the dirt floor as she said, "The *bayle* and his men found Éléonore, Alesta, and their whole family dead. They had eaten mushroom soup. Éléonore knew her mushrooms well, so it wasn't an accident. Now Perter is the only one still left alive from that house. But he'll hang at the Devil's Doorstep before the next full moon."

Bertwoin put a hand on the cold oven to steady himself. "How could she have done this?"

The master watched the lumps attentively without answering, his face as morose as someone visiting a loved one's new grave.

Flowia sighed. "They had almost starved to death when Perter fled to the mountains to avoid your father. Now he lies in the dungeon. Who would feed them?" She balled up a fist and shook it, her face twisted with anger. "Why is it that the women and children must always be the ones who suffer for the sins of the fathers?"

"But Éléonore will never lie in hallowed ground," Bertwoin said. "None of them will. The Church will judge them as suicides."

Flowia shrugged. "No matter. She didn't believe most of the Church's teachings. Their consecrated ground was no holier to her than marshland. She probably thought it was best for all of them to start new lives. She decided to let God, not the Church, judge them."

Bertwoin made the sign of the cross. "As you once told me, revenge often turns against the one who seeks it. Éléonore destroyed her whole family."

The master seemed so intent on his process that he wasn't listening to them. Curious as a pig, Bertwoin ambled over to see what was so interesting. Like monsters underwater, the two orange lumps were sprouting tendrils.

Bertwoin said to Flowia, "Now I can't help Alesta. I can't return the kindness she showed me." He spread his hands. "Why would she not stay alive? She knew that once she was gone, Perter had no one to bring him food or drink."

"Ah, but that may be one of the tendrils of this growing tragedy," the master said. "Éléonore may have poisoned her entire family without any of them knowing it. She thought death was an easier fate for her children than starvation."

Bertwoin's nose burned, and he fought to keep tears from forming in his eyes.

"And you might still return the favor to Alesta," Flowia told him.

Both men looked at her. "You can take food to her husband."

"Me?" he blurted out. "He'll think I bring him poison."

231

"If that were so," the master said, "it could be considered a kindness. The butcher might even eat it willingly and thank you for the gift. Some poisons are easy deaths."

The alchemist cleared his throat. "And let us not throw stones only at Éléonore and Perter. Alesta, I think, made the poisoned lark you saw in the Arundel's kitchen. The knot was fashioned by her, not her mother. It was she who killed the seneschal's son."

"Ah," said Bertwoin. "Éléonore's crippled hands."

"Yes," the alchemist agreed. "Tying delicate knots was beyond her ability. And was it not Alesta who looked so proud when you complimented the skill used in making their bird net?"

"One thing still puzzles me," Bertwoin said, fascinated as he watched a long, orange tendril grow toward the surface of the clear, syrupy liquid. "Why did Perter leave Master Servay's rotting head at Tisbe's? It was certain to be found."

Flowia set a wet beaker on the table for Bertwoin to dry. "Oh, they wanted it found."

"True," the master said. "And we will never know the reason for certain, but I believe it was a brazen hint as to what this murder was all about. Éléonore had lost a son, so Sir Jean-Luc must also lose a son. And the seneschal's whore, as the Château Comtal ladies called her, took delight in Sir Jean-Luc finding his son's head in a *whore's* room."

"If they had hidden everything and kept quiet," Bertwoin said, "we might never have proved they did it."

"Ah well," the master said. "Revenge is doubled if the victim knows who claimed it and why. That is also the reason Perter let you know that he had fed Master Servay's flesh to his father. The seneschal had to be told."

The alchemist coughed. "And speaking of being found, two days from now you won't find me here. I'm to accompany *Visconte* Raimon-Rogièr to Albi. Murder, it seems, doesn't happen only in Carcassonne. The *visconte* needs my investigative skills there."

Bertwoin glanced at Flowia. They would be alone together for at least a few days, and he felt only a twinge of guilt about the fact that he was eager for the master's absence.

CHAPTER XXXII.

While sitting at supper a day after the alchemist had left for Albi, Clanoud announced he was going to open up more forest ground for barley. When his wife dared asked why he would want to do that since they had all the fieldwork they could handle and then some, he slapped her, bringing tears to her eyes.

"Don't ever gainsay me again, woman."

Bertwoin blew out his breath as he put his hands flat on the table and slowly shoved himself to standing. Surprised, Clanoud looked up from where he sat on a stool and sneered at his son's righteous anger.

"No more," Bertwoin said.

Clanoud appraised his son, his eyes shining with amused surprise and maybe a trace of respect. "Boy, I keep order in this household. Watch how you talk to me lest I make you suffer for it."

"There's no fat on me," Bertwoin said, his voice a rasp of anger.

Wilfraed stared at his brother as if Saint Nazarius had come to him in a vision. Ellyn stood up and moved away with her eyes aimed at the rushes on the floor. His sisters and even his uncle were too shocked to move from the table.

Clanoud looked askance at his wife. "You think he can protect you, Ellyn? It's not like you to let him take a beating for you."

"He shouldn't have to," she said. "Protecting me is for you to do."

"A beating, Ellyn."

"He'll give a good account of himself," she said. "He's like you, strong and won't quit. No mule can out-stubborn him. Next week, he'll fight you again and the week after that. And if you're not careful, you won't have him to plow for you."

Clanoud wiped the knife he was using to eat on a piece of bread and shoved the blade in the sheath hanging from his belt. "There ain't but twelve or thirteen men in this village who can best me, and I include unarmed knights and men-at-arms." He stood up, staying on the other side of the table from his eldest son.

Bertwoin's brother and sisters scattered along the walls farthest away from the kitchen table, their eyes wide with awe. His Uncle Laurence slid off the bench and stood near his sister-in-law. Everyone in the room knew Clanoud would win.

Bertwoin too was resigned to this fact. He would take a beating, but he intended to sell himself dear so his father would think twice before hitting his *maman* again.

Bertwoin said, "Women and children shouldn't have to suffer because of the sins of the father."

Everyone gaped at him, except for his *maman*. She picked up a knife half as long as her forearm and looked her husband in the eye, her threat as plain as sunlight.

Clanoud asked, "Do you think he can run this farm?"

"If we don't open up more ground because of your peasant pride," she said. "And without him," she nodded at Bertwoin, "you'll not be ridding the woods of many tree stumps."

Clanoud laughed without joy. "Well, now I know how it all stands." He looked with haughty contempt at his son. "You'll change your ways after you take a wife. And you *wiU* clear and plow me a new acre, butt-crack. Don't make any mistake about that."

Clanoud turned and strode out through the open front door, passing by his wife as if she held a spindle instead of a knife. Once outside, they all heard him begin to whistle the tune of a troubadour's *canso*.

Bertwoin wiped the sweat off his forehead. He felt as tired as if he had plowed a drought-hard field. Was his father pleased that his eldest son had shown out as a man or was he even now chuckling at the revenge he would claim for this rebellion?

One fact was certain: his father hadn't walked away because of fear. He would fight, even if he knew he'd lose. Probably he decided that beating his eldest son senseless again and again wasn't worth the cost. Bertwoin needed to be healthy and whole for the coming plowing season.

"Everyone sit down and finish your supper," Ellyn said. Without raising her eyes to Bertwoin, she laid the knife on a table and went out to her husband.

Later that evening, she found Bertwoin alone in the barn and told him to go to the master's house and ask if he could sleep there for a while.

"You're throwing me out?"

She patted his arm. "No, Bertwoin, I'm not. That was a brave thing you did. I would never punish you for it. But two full-grown roosters in the same yard will rip each other apart until neither of them is worth having. You know your father. I'll send one of the girls when I judge it time for you to come back. You do know, though, that you'll have to clear the extra land for him?"

"I didn't balk him over that."

She kissed his cheek. "I know. Get the things you need and go ask permission."

His *maman* didn't know that the master alchemist was still in Albi as part of *Visconte* Raimon-Rogièr's entourage, and he didn't tell her. Having his *maman's* permission to stay with Flowia while she was alone, if Flowia allowed it, was a gift from heaven. He hoped that the fact he had decided to not be like his father in all things would help persuade Flowia to let him stay with her.

If you enjoyed *The Wrathful Cup of Scorn*, please consider leaving a review. Other than buying an author's book, this is the most precious gift a reader can give an author.